The Lighthouse Thief

The Lighthouse Thief

Bo Burnette

illustrated by Josiah Dooley

The Lighthouse Thief
Copyright © 2014 Bo Burnette
Published by Tabbystone Press

T abbystone P ress

Scripture quotations are from The Holy Bible, English Standard Version® (ESV®), copyright © 2001 by Crossway, a publishing ministry of Good News Publishers. Used by permission. All rights reserved.

All illustrations were rendered in pencil by Josiah Dooley, except for the text message illustrations, which were created by Bo Burnette.

The cover font "Conspiracy" is © 2001 Nerfect Type Laboratories and Britton Walters.

ISBN-13: 978-0985061234
ISBN-10: 0985061235

First Edition
Printed and bound in the United States
Also available in eBook editions

To Grand and Papa Jim,
Thanks for all the great times and amazing memories!

TABLE OF CONTENTS

Prologue

Life is something of a paradox. Some things that we aspire to so highly as our chief goals become only slightly satisfying once we attain them; yet many things we dismiss as unimportant are really the most significant. With one tiny decision, you can change a day, a lifetime, a destiny.

I didn't mean to get entangled in any trouble this summer. I really didn't.

But I did.

It was a series of those tiny but important decisions. Still, I suppose it wasn't quite what one would call *trouble*. It really turned out to be rather good. All adventures have their troublesome spots, though.

I had better introduce myself. My name is Ethan Lewis. I'm fourteen and have sandy brown hair made lighter by time in the coastal Georgia sun.

It all started when I invited my cousin from Chicago to spend a week with me at my house on Saint Simons Island. I was planning a nice, leisurely week with a little sightseeing and stuff like that. I had it all precisely laid out. I like things that way—I'm a pretty exact person.

But this July, I found out that things don't always go as planned.

Chapter One:
Four Reasons

SWISH. SWISH. I opened my eyes a sliver, hearing the live oaks brushing their boughs of Spanish moss against my bedroom window on the second floor. I glanced at the clock. It was 7:29 a.m. Turning my head around, I glanced toward the window. As on most Saturdays, the neighborhood was quiet. Everyone was sleeping in, but somehow I couldn't this morning. I liked it this way every once in a while, feeling like I was the only person awake in my corner of the world. A gentle breeze made a tall oak outside again sweep its branches dripping with moss against my windowpane. The sun, still low in the sky, beamed through this canopy.

I swiveled my head back around, and found another set of eyes staring into mine. My dog Summer sat by my bed, her tail wagging and swishing like a horse's. Grinning sleepily, I stroked her fluffy head.

I rose noiselessly and crept down the stairs with Summer at my heels. All was still in our sprawling two-story house, and my footsteps squeaked on the slick, polished wooden stairs.

After reading my Bible, I went into the kitchen, poured a bowl of cereal, and plunked myself on the couch, glancing at the stack of magazines on the coffee table. I quietly began to sort through them to find something interesting. Suddenly one caught my eye — a gray brochure which read: "History is waiting! We invite you to climb, wander, see, hear, touch, explore, experience, and enjoy it all!"

I pulled the brochure out of the stack of magazines. "Coastal Georgia Historical Society," it said, and a picture of the Saint Simons Island Lighthouse graced the front cover. I scanned the brochure, which was full of information about the lighthouse. I'd visited it many times, so many that I had the light (as we Islanders sometimes refer to it) memorized by heart. Still, the brochure had some new information I'd never heard before. I was so absorbed in the booklet that I didn't hear Mom walk down the stairs and into the living room.

"Good morning, Ethan," she greeted me. "You're up early." I lowered the pamphlet to find her in front of me.

"Morning, Mom," I jumped up and gave her a quick hug.

"I got an email from your Aunt Emma last night. She's going to be coming to stay with you when Dad and I go on our trip with Aunt Suzanne and Uncle Gary," she said. I already figured that Aunt Emma would be the one to stay with me, for it seemed she always had been, and always would be, my babysitter. (Such a peculiar word, since half the time the kids that the babysitter is watching aren't even babies. And what about the sitter part? Aunt Emma never *sat* on me, and we never just *sat* around when she was here.) I loved Aunt Emma, my great-aunt. I loved her kind, quirky sweetness and her youthful spirit. Spending time with her, whether helping her in her little garden or going on trips with her, was always a treat.

Anyway, Mom and Dad had been planning their one-week trip to Alaska for many months now. It would be a short — and cool — getaway from The Island.

"So, what did Aunt Emma say?" I asked.

Mom continued, "She suggested that you invite your cousin Connor to come and stay with you here, since his parents will be away with us. He'd be great company, and you two could catch up a little bit. She said she'd love to have her two great-nephews for a week."

"Connor?" I raised an eyebrow. "Honestly?"

Connor—who lived in Chicago—wasn't exactly my favorite cousin, and often we didn't get along well. Although we knew each other fairly well and been together at several family gatherings, our relationship never drifted into the realm of true friendship. He had always seemed a bit cold and closed to me. There were, of course, many other reasons for this. Some reasons I wouldn't even realize until much later.

"What would be wrong with it, Ethan? I know you two aren't the best of friends, but maybe you could get to know each other a little better if he came."

"He doesn't want to get to know me, Mom. I'm sure of it."

"Perhaps that's because you haven't tried to get to know him," she replied.

"I'm with Mom on this one, Ethan." Dad's sudden appearance in the living room surprised us both. "It would be great for both of you."

"Yes, sir," I relented, grimacing slightly. "I'll call him now."

I punched Connor's number into my cell phone.

The phone rang for a long time. I took a swig from my glass of water and waited. Summer, sitting beside me expectantly, panted happily when I started petting her golden locks. I think she could sense my uneasiness—my irritation. Growing impatient, I was about to hang up when someone finally answered.

"Hi. May I speak to Connor?" I asked.

"This is Connor," he said slowly from the other end.

"Oh...Hi. This is Ethan." I waited for his response.

"Hi, Ethan," Connor didn't sound as if my phone call was making his day any better.

I took a deep breath. "Good morning."

"A little early for a Saturday, isn't it?" he said groggily. Then I realized that his time was an hour earlier than mine. I did a mental facepalm and then continued.

"Sorry—I forgot about the time zones. I just wanted to invite you to spend a week with me down at The Island. Nothing fancy—just with Aunt Emma while our parents are in Alaska." There was a brief silence on the other end.

"Um...okay," he said. "And what would we be doing? Anything at all interesting?"

"Come on, Connor! I've visited you in Chicago, like, twice! You owe it to me."

Connor paused for a moment. "Listen, Ethan. I have all the best stuff up here: great food, historic landmarks, and everything else. And the pizza! I'll bet you don't have pizza anything like here in Chicago." He paused a moment. When I didn't speak, he continued. "So I have a deal for you: give me three good reasons why I should come to your little island. If they're good, I'll come, and if I come, you have to prove those reasons to me. Deal?"

"Deal," I said hesitantly, and Summer cocked her head curiously. I searched my mind for the three most convincing reasons why he should come. I knew they were there somewhere, I just had to extract them from the depths of my mind.

"Okay, Connor. Here you go:

Number one: we have all sorts of cool historic landmarks and sights, including Fort Frederica and the Saint Simons Lighthouse.

Number two: there are great beaches for hanging out and all sorts of water sports.

Number three: you'll love the feel of The Island — the locally-owned shops and restaurants, the low-hanging trees covered with Spanish moss, the friendly people; I could go on and on...

You didn't ask for number four, but I'll give it anyway. It may sound weird, but just know that if you come to Saint Simons, you'll never be the same."

I finished my reasons with a dramatic pause, hoping to persuade him. Connor was once again silent.

"Ethan, listen," he said. I braced myself for a resounding 'no.' However, it did not come. "My answer is 'Yes,' Ethan. I want to see if your reasons are really true — especially number four. So I'll come. I think that I'm ready for your island. But your island had better be ready for me."

Chapter Two:
Stony Hearts

Thursday, June 30, was a rotten day to oversleep. But, it happens to the best of us.

That's right. The morning my parents were leaving for Alaska *and* my cousin was arriving, I slept half an hour late. So, instead of seven a.m., bright and early, I awoke at seven thirty-two. When I sleepily trudged down the stairs, my parents were already dressed and ready, bustling about the kitchen. Summer scuttled about, sniffing the floor to see if any crumbs had been dropped in their rush.

"Ethan, you should have been up an hour ago!" Mom scolded, hastily stuffing a bag of coffee into her suitcase. "Connor's flight arrives at 9:25, and our flight departs at 10:20. We need to leave fairly soon." I nodded and hurriedly dressed and ate my breakfast—barely having time to snag a quick cup of much-needed coffee. After this, it was off to the Brunswick airport.

Brunswick was the town on the Georgia mainland nearest to The Island, but from our house on the northern end of Saint Simons, it took a good while to get there. As we drove, I gazed at the buildings which zoomed by. I had lived here all my life, so everything had personal meaning to me. Even the age-old oaks with their lofty limbs held a special place in my mind. The trees of Saint Simons provided a matchless atmosphere and veiled The Island's roads with enchanting shadows. As the sun began to ascend higher in the sky, the trees began to draw up their flickering silhouettes.

Saint Simons Island had been a part of my family for a long time. Many of my relatives lived on The Island, including my Aunt Emma, and my mom's sister and her family — which included my cousin, Cassidy. Cassidy and I were close friends and had always been chums, since we were born only a month apart. We got along perfectly: both of us possessed talkative, opinionated, fun-loving spirits. If only it was *her* spending the week instead of Connor...but that was an unkind thought. And I knew unkind thoughts were not going to make matters any better, so I shoved it out of my mind and continued looking out the window.

The Torras Causeway, which spanned the marshes and rivers between The Island and the mainland, consisted of a series of bridges. We crossed the final bridge that yoked The Island to the mainland — the city of Brunswick. When we arrived at the airport, we found Aunt Emma already waiting next to her sparkly, lime-green Volkswagen beetle.

"Hey there! I thought that you'd never arrive, Will," Aunt Emma said to Dad. "I've been waiting here for nearly half an hour." My dad smiled.

"I know you're always early, Aunt Emma," he replied, hugging her. She, in turn, planted a kiss on his cheek. Aunt Emma now turned to me.

"How's my great-nephew? As fidgety as ever, I see," she said, giving me a quick hug. "Let me guess — you can't wait for Connor to get here?" I rolled my eyes. Aunt Emma knew how Connor and I felt about each other, and she couldn't resist teasing me. "Don't worry," she assured me with a whisper, "I have everything under control." She winked a wise, blue eye.

The small yet surprisingly upscale terminal was bustling with travelers on their way to and from the majestic Golden Isles. Once inside, I scanned the crowds for Connor. He would be flying alone from Atlanta, where his parents had dropped him off after their flight from Chicago. Mom and Dad would be flying to Atlanta, and from there on to Alaska with my aunt and uncle. I imagined how much fun it would be if I was at the airport to travel somewhere else, flying off on an amazing journey. Once I thought about it, I realized how much I really wanted an adventure. Although living off your imagination is fine, nothing beats a real adventure.

Suddenly, I snapped to attention when I saw Connor walking toward us, rolling a single suitcase. He wore a faded green t-shirt and jeans. I took a deep breath. *Here goes nothing*, I told myself. Aunt Emma immediately recognized Connor and grabbed him in a hug.

"My two great-nephews for a week—how exciting is that?" she exclaimed. Connor smiled slightly at Aunt Emma, but his dark brown eyes revealed the obvious: he wasn't terribly thrilled. In fact, he looked sort of bored as he swished his dark hair to the side. *Great*, I thought, *Typical. Oh well, he could be worse.* Mom must have read my thoughts, because she elbowed me and whispered, "Say 'hi' or something. You should be polite to your guest."

"Um, hi," I mumbled. Connor didn't say anything, he only nodded his head. Suddenly my dad gasped. "It's already almost ten—we need to hurry so we don't miss our flight." He gave me a giant hug. "Love you, Ethan. Take care of yourself and have a good Fourth of July."

"Thanks, Dad," I smiled. Then came my mom.

"Bye, Ethan," she said, hugging me. Then she stepped back and, gripping my shoulders firmly, said, "You and Connor need to learn to understand each other. You must win him not only with The Island, but with the kindness of your actions and words. Those matter more than where you live or what you can offer him."

I paused hesitantly, and she continued. "I want you to have this. I love you, Ethan." She pressed something small firmly into my hand, then turned and left. I glanced at the object. It was a small key chain with a charm in the shape and color of the St. Simons Lighthouse. I gripped it and waved goodbye to my parents as they walked toward the security gates.

"Come on, boys," Aunt Emma said. "Adventure awaits us!"

And right then, a good lunch sounded like adventure to me.

"I'm not sure about most of your four reasons, but the part about restaurants is definitely right," Connor commented after finishing another slice of pizza. "It's different, but practically as good as it is in..." his voice trailed off when he saw my smirk.

We were at CJ's, my favorite local pizza joint on The Island. I grinned, wiping pizza sauce off the corner of my mouth. Connor seemed to be warming up to The Island already. I had cast my line, and he had fallen for the bait—hook, line, and sinker. The pizza was perfect, with a delicious crust, crispy bacon, and a generous helping of melty cheese. Taking a swig of Coke, I drained my almost-empty glass. A waitress, noticing, came by and refilled it.

"How many Cokes have you had, Ethan?" Aunt Emma said with amused suspicion.

"Um...three, I think," I replied. She laughed merrily, but Connor snickered.

"Don't drink too many, pig!" he teased.

"How many have you had?" I returned. He was silent. "Touché, eh?"

Aunt Emma raised her own glass of Coke. "A toast to our week together!" She said.

Back at home, Connor and I looked over my plan of what I wanted to do with him that week. (As I said earlier, I had it all planned out to make Connor want to believe my reasons. However, I ignored a few small details. Small details often cause big changes.)

"This is yours...I have another list for myself." I handed him the small sheet of notebook paper.

"Thanks," Connor muttered as he accepted the slip of paper.

It was around one o'clock in the afternoon, and we were sitting on my bed poring over the list. A beam of sunlight streamed through the top of the window into my face, and I shifted positions to avoid the glare.

Then, as Connor wasn't saying anything, I broke the silence by reading the items on the list aloud:

1. Visit lighthouse and Maritime Center
2. Tour Fort Frederica monument
3. Go to beach
4. Visit the shops in the village
5. See fireworks on the 4th at the
   pier
6. kayak
7. See a movie at the theater
8. Etc.

"Sound good to you?" I asked.

"I guess," he said. "But so far, you haven't really fulfilled any of your four reasons."

"Thanks for reminding me," I replied sarcastically. Connor seemed to ignore my comment.

"So," he said in a patronizing tone, "when does my 'oh-so-special-grand-tour' of your island begin?"

I snapped my head toward him. "Could you quit talking like that? I'm sick of you whining and complaining all the time." I paused, glaring.

"Oh yeah?" he shot back with equal enthusiasm. "When's the last time you did anything to me besides bossing and ordering me around? Huh, Ethan?" We both stood up. I was not much taller than Connor—only about an inch.

"I wish I had just stayed up in Chicago!" he stated a bit loudly.

"I wish you had, too!" I returned. "But now you're here, and you're wrecking my week!"

Connor stepped closer, but was interrupted by a sudden presence in the room. Aunt Emma stepped toward us, her thin eyebrows raised slightly.

"Now boys, we don't need to start our week off by fighting, do we? I say let's settle this calmly, then go see a movie. It's best to start good times off on a high note, isn't it?" She turned around to leave the room. "I'll be ready in ten minutes—and you two had better be, too." Then she left. I turned to Connor.

"I—I'm sorry…" I began, but Connor cut me off.

"I'm sorry, too," he retorted, "Sorry that I ever came here!" He turned on his heel and left. I was left alone in my bedroom, wondering how I could soften a stony heart. Then my thoughts froze. Was there one stony heart, or two?

Chapter Three:
129 Steps, 1 Mystery

"...Ninety-one, ninety-two, ninety-three, ninety-four, ninety-five," I counted. I was counting steps—all one hundred twenty-nine steps up the St. Simons Lighthouse. I glanced over my shoulder at Connor. He seemed to be enjoying himself, but it was hard to interpret any emotion from the stolid expression on his face. After all, he had only just arrived yesterday. I sighed but kept counting the iron stairs.

"...one hundred twenty-seven, one hundred twenty-eight, one hundred twenty-nine!" I exclaimed as we reached the top. Aunt Emma had stayed behind and let both of us go on. "I've walked up that thing a billion times before," she had said with a laugh. "You two go ahead."

Now, at the top, I hesitated before going through the open door. I hoped the beautiful panoramic view of the beach and pier would impress Connor. Incredible views always impressed me—even took my breath away. I hoped that Connor was the same way.

I slipped through the doorway and we both stepped into the light of the midmorning sun. I'd been up here before, but each time I was overtaken by the view. It was a perfectly clear day, so the view stretched to the grassy lawn far below, then to the pier, the ocean, and beyond that—the horizon. I breathed in the fresh, salty air and sighed. This was Saint Simons; this was home.

Connor, too, seemed to enjoy it. I glanced his way and almost gasped in surprise. Connor was smiling. For the first time since he'd arrived here, he was truly, genuinely smiling. However, he glanced my way, and immediately his smile vanished. Wishing to revive his joyful spirit, I walked over in his direction. I gripped the iron handrail beside him.

"It's a beautiful view, isn't it?" I said dreamily.

"Beauty is in the eye of the beholder," Connor replied coolly, then added, "But it is a pretty view." I turned away. Quite frankly, I wanted to smash his indifferent face into the iron rails. Praying a quick request for extra patience, I took a deep breath and restrained my hard feelings, letting the warm air flow into my lungs. My thoughts turned to other things.

The lighthouse stands like a great pillar, a landmark on the far tip of The Island. It seems to be as much a citizen of Saint Simons as any of the islanders themselves are, for it has seen long years of history since it replaced its original counterpart in 1872. While the soft sands of the beach lie not too far away, the light tower itself is made of and stands on a foundation of firm *tabby* — a coastal material made of limestone and oyster shells. The tower's color is white, or perhaps a faded cream, especially when the sky is darker. Situated upon the top of the tabby-stone tower is a small, glass-enclosed chamber containing a lens which magnifies the bright beam of light. On the exterior of this glass chamber is a balcony, surrounded by a thick iron handrail. From this vantage point, one can see the lighthouse stretching down to the ground below, and in the near distance the ocean throws its waves against the beach. Even farther away lie other islands, and, beyond that, the water stretches to the horizon.

I could see most of the south end of The Island from my high vantage. I thought back to former days, when the lighthouse saw much more use as a guide and warning to incoming ships. James Gould, a brilliant architect from Massachusetts, made his home on Saint Simons and built the original lighthouse in

1810. However, history took its toll on the structure; Confederate troops destroyed it during the Civil War to hinder the Union troops from using it. Thankfully, the light had been rebuilt—the same tower that I stood on, enjoying the view.

I was about to start walking around the balcony when I saw two men on the other side of the railed platform that circled the lighthouse. A taller man was holding a piece of paper and glancing upward at the part of the lighthouse from which the light shone at night. A shorter man was staring at the taller man's notepad, and both were talking in low whispers. While Connor continued to take in the scenery, I ducked barely out of sight of the men but stayed just close enough to listen to their whispered conversation.

"So, you say it's valuable?" the shorter man asked slowly.

"Of course, you ninny!" the taller man whispered. "It's an original Fresnel lens. That's why we have to be so careful not to...damage it if it becomes involved. It shouldn't be—"

"How do you say that word again?" the shorter interrupted.

"FREH-nel," the taller said in a raspy voice. "Stop asking so many questions. You talk too loudly, and you never know who else is listening."

I realized this could be important and whipped out my notepad. I was rarely without my notepad. Whether for making to-do lists, taking note of important goings-on, or writing down random thoughts, I found a notepad to be an irreplaceable tool. Ducking just out of their sight, I continued listening to their conversation and scribbled down:

- Two men whispering about the lighthouse lens
- Valuable Fresnel lens
- Pronounced FREH-nel

Hmm, I thought to myself, *That sounds as fishy as a fresh catch from the ocean.* I laughed silently at my inaudible—and ridiculous—pun.

Connor rounded the corner and faced me. "Well, it's a pretty nice lighthouse, I guess. Didn't Aunt Emma used to work here or something?"

"Yep," I answered. "She volunteered here for a long time. I could come up here any time I wanted."

"Seriously—any time?"

"I guess I could come up here any time...I mean, I never asked to come up after hours or anything. Though I've always wanted to come up here for the fireworks show..."

"You could do that? I mean, when Aunt Emma worked here?"

"How should I know?" I shrugged.

He wrinkled his nose and shrugged as well. "Ready to go?" he asked.

"Oh, yeah. Let's go," I said a bit too loudly. The taller man, who had obviously thought they were alone, peered around the corner and stared at me straight in the face. He had small, dark eyes, and a long nose that flared as he grimaced at me. I grabbed Connor's arm and led him quickly down the flight of stairs. I didn't even bother to count them—the man's glare had struck me with a sudden feeling of fear.

"Let go!" he ordered once we were headed down. "Are you okay?"

"I'm fine...I just thought...we needed to, um, get back to Aunt Emma," I replied.

We found Aunt Emma browsing the lighthouse museum store. "Finally back, you two? Ready to go on to Fort Frederica?" Connor nodded, but said he needed to use the restroom. Aunt Emma went too, and I was left alone, sitting on the bench in the hallway. Light streamed cheerily into the room from sections of glass walls on either side. There was a model of the ship *U.S.S. Constitution* on display, because live oak trees from Saint Simons had been used in its building.

I pulled out my notepad to examine the things I had written. I love good detective stories every once in a while, and couldn't stand to pass up this mystery. It seemed intriguing enough. Suddenly, I heard the two men from the lighthouse standing just around the corner talking. I readied my pencil, listening for any clues to this strange puzzle.

Obviously, the tall, thin man was oblivious I was eavesdropping. His resonant voice carried around the corner and into the sunny hall, so I could hear some of the conversation distinctly. "It's really simple, Ben," the tall, thin man was saying, "Everyone will be enjoying the Independence Day fireworks. There will be plenty of time, so it's going to all go according to the plan. We'll get in and get out in no time. And if all goes well with our inspection..."

The huskier man named Ben nodded, running his fingers through his blond hair. "You certainly make it sound easy! You are pretty smart, Winston."

Winston rolled his eyes. "Yes, and you're just pretty stupid. Remember I'm in charge of this whole thing—you're just here to assist me. Things will have to be done very carefully...and quietly." He continued, "Today's Friday. We have three more days until the 4th — Monday — so we'd better get cracking. We have work to do."

I couldn't believe what I had just heard. Were these men simply inspectors, or were they up to something? They were walking away now, and Aunt Emma and Connor had just come out of the bathroom.

"Let's go, my charges!" Aunt Emma said loudly. At her loud interjection, the two men turned and stared at us. Winston, the tall one, peered around and stared at me the same way he had on top of the lighthouse. His stare told me one thing: he guessed that I guessed he was up to something.

Chapter Four:
Choices at Fort Frederica

The moment we got in the car, Connor bombarded me with questions. "Why were you staring at that tall guy? What were you writing in that notepad? What's going on?!"

Aunt Emma had the radio turned up loudly. She drummed her thumbs on the steering wheel in time with the music, paying little attention to Connor and me. I turned to Connor.

"Okay, it's sort of hard to explain. But I think I've just uncovered a major plot—like the kind you read about in books. Those two guys...here, just read my notes," I handed the small yellow notepad to Connor. He scrutinized my hurried handwriting.

- Two men whispering about the lighthouse lens
- Valuable Fresnel lens
- Pronounced FREH-nel
- Men plotting to steal something? Or just inspectors?
- Names: Ben & Winston (taller man)
- Planning to do something secretly during the fireworks show on Monday night!

Connor looked up at me. I expected him to be fascinated at a mystery to solve, but his face only revealed a mocking expression. "Come on, Ethan. You can't be serious," he began. "These men have got to be talking about something else, so stop your little detective game. You've just misheard some normal adults having a normal conversation. After all, it's not nice to eavesdrop, is it?" Connor turned away and stared out his window. I yanked on his sleeve.

"This is serious," I hissed. "I promise that I'm not fooling around. Just trust me! I think those guys might be really trying to steal *something* — I just don't know exactly what."

"Come on, Ethan," he said. "Be real. They're probably just inspectors or something." He turned back to stare out the window.

I sighed. I felt like I always sighed when Connor was around; he was just so difficult to talk to. Pushing away my annoyance, I focused on our current destination: the Fort Frederica monument, which lay on the northern end of The Island. I hoped it would not bore Connor. I didn't think it would, since he was a bit of a history buff, and quite fascinated with military and historic battles. The fort was certainly rich with history and tales of times bygone.

My mind kept drifting back to the incident at the lighthouse. It was all very puzzling. Perhaps Connor really was right...

My thoughts were suddenly halted as we pulled up at Fort Frederica. Aunt Emma shifted into park and opened her car door. "Come on, boys! Let's explore!" I stepped from the car and slammed the door shut. *I'm tired of exploring*, I thought. *No...that's not it — I'm tired of Connor!* Then I remembered: If I was ever going to get him to see my four reasons, stony hearts had to be softened. Two stony hearts.

I slipped my hand into my pocket and felt the lighthouse keychain my mom had given me before she left. *"You must win him not only with The Island, but with your actions and words,"* she had said. I determined to do just that.

Connor and Aunt Emma were already walking up to the Visitor's Center which prefaced the main attraction. "Hurry up, Ethan!" Aunt Emma called. I obeyed and sprinted up to where they were. We entered a small building, and, after buying tickets, continued on to see Fort Frederica.

Frederica had once been a major military town. Founded in the 1730s as a chief protector of Britain's claims in colonial Georgia, it had been the site of the Battle of Bloody Marsh, in which General James Oglethorpe's British troops defeated the Spaniards. But now, centuries later, Frederica lay in ruins. The tabbystone and brick foundations of many houses still remained, but the largest ruins were that of the ancient barracks, and the old fort itself. Aunt Emma led the way down a side road, called Cross Street, and we entered the remains of the barracks. Once inside the ruins of the old fort, Connor became quiet. He seemed happy, and I was glad that I didn't have to defend this part of "my little island."

We were standing in the doorway of a former tower. The tabbystone structure looked old enough to fall apart. Each part of the ruins was old, crumbling, and yet unique. I knew that each stone had a story to tell about Saint Simons' rich history.

The afternoon sun bore down on the scantily shaded area. When I was about to ask what the time was, I saw a sight which seemed to make my heart stop beating. There, standing at the end of Cross Street, were Winston and Ben, staring at me from a distance. I turned my head and pretended not to notice they were there. However, I couldn't put them out of my mind.

Why didn't I just ignore them when I heard them on the lighthouse? I thought to myself. Then I realized that the answer was simple: I believed my four reasons for loving Saint Simons, and if something of the lighthouse was stolen...well, I just felt I had to protect it. I glanced over in Connor's direction, and suddenly I realized he had seen Winston and Ben, too. I gave him a smirk that said, "Told you so!" and he shot back with a grimace that said, "Smarty-pants!"

I couldn't smile for long, though. This was no time for sarcastic teasing — there were two strange men with a potentially terrible plot, and they seemed to be after me, almost like spies. This was serious. I had a choice: I could tell Aunt Emma, and she might call the police and end everything (or maybe they wouldn't even believe us), or I could wait a little and find out how much of this was real.

I decided on the second choice. It certainly wouldn't be any fun if grown-ups got involved, would it? They probably wouldn't help. They probably wouldn't believe me. I would find out later that this was a bad idea, but you cannot always know what will happen in the future when making a choice. We continued touring the old town, but my mind—and eyes—kept drifting back to our secret pursuers. I couldn't even focus on the highlight of our trip, the fort itself.

The aged fort occupied a place right on the edge of the marshy Frederica River. I genuinely wished to jump straight into the brackish water. It was a brutally hot day, and perspiration rolled down my forehead. Although Saint Simons summers could be breezily pleasant, they also had their sweltering days— especially when the wind died down.

"All right, boys. I'm terribly hot, and we've seen it all. Let's go, Ethan. Come on, Connor," Aunt Emma gripped her purse. We strode down the main road, Broad Street, toward the Visitor's Center and parking lot. Suddenly I noticed the gift shop, the centerpiece of which was a shelf packed with Saint Simons books.

"Um, Aunt Emma, could I take a look in the store really quickly?" I interjected.

"Go ahead," she replied. "But make it quick. I'll be right out here."

I handed Connor my blue backpack to hold as I left. He and Aunt Emma sat on a bench, and Connor plunked my backpack down beside him.

I scanned the bookshelf, looking for an intriguing title. A few books stood out markedly—like one titled *Georgia's Land of the Golden Isles*. The author, Burnette Vanstory, was unfamiliar to me, but the book stood beside a paperback of Eugenia Price's

Lighthouse — a novel I knew well. Suddenly, I realized Aunt Emma was waving for me to come. I left the shelf empty-handed.

Outside, I observed that Connor looked as if he had seen a ghost.

"Are you all right, Connor?" I asked. He nodded uneasily and pointed to the yellow notebook in my pocket. I now knew what he was talking about. I chose the backseat of the car again. I wanted Connor to be able to tell me everything. In the car, I buckled and looked outside. There, sitting in a black Honda, were Winston and Ben, watching until we were out of sight.

Chapter Five:
The Plot Thickens

In the backseat, I didn't even have to ask Connor to fill me in. He began right away.

"Aunt Emma and I were talking about the kayaking trip she's planned for us tomorrow." he said in a low voice. "And...and I think that tall guy—"

"Winston," I cut Connor off.

"Yeah, Winston. Well, he was passing by. And I think heard me, 'cause he gave me this creepy look—like, a really creepy look. I think he was eavesdropping, but I just didn't realize it at first. He heard all about our plans for tomorrow, and I'm beginning to think you might be right that they're up to something."

I paused. "Connor, why are you telling me this? I thought you didn't want to have anything to do with this mystery. I thought you weren't even interested in this island!"

"Well..." he replied hesitantly, "You've already proved to me reason number one: 'there are all sorts of cool historic landmarks and sights.' The fort was pretty awesome. I feel like I at least owe you that."

I smiled slightly at his seemingly changed heart.

Then he spoke again, in a less forgiving tone: "But don't expect me to help you a bunch anymore. I told you this one thing, because you proved one reason to me. I'm still not getting involved with this mystery. And about the reasons part—I think you still have a long way to go. Remember the deal?"

Turning around toward the window, I glanced up at the towering oaks and sighed. It seemed like things would never change. Unexpectedly, a Bible verse from John came to my mind: *"I am the light of the world. Whoever follows me will not walk in darkness, but will have the light of life."* Jesus' words about light resonated with me in regard to the lighthouse. I understood what my mom had meant. It was my duty to treat Connor with love and kindness, and to be—in a way—a sort of lighthouse. I resolved for this to be my purpose.

It was 8:00 a.m.—a nice, breezy Saturday morning on Saint Simons, perfect for kayaking. And that was exactly what we were planning. Knowing we would want something interesting to do, Aunt Emma had scheduled a tour for all three of us. The tours went in groups of around five to fifteen people, and were led by an expert kayaker tour guide.

We were not going to be kayaking in the open ocean, but in the marshy area where thick layers of thin-bladed grasses seemed to make small rivers and channels in the salty water. It was in the middle of The Island—halfway between my house on the north end and the Village and pier on the south end—where the best spots were to put out to sea for fishing. I glanced over the marsh from the gently sloping hill where I stood. The water, flowing gently, was calm and serene. A cobblestone pavement led down the incline and into the water, providing a place to drop off one's boat for a trip around the marshlands. In the distance I saw two large birds flying over the tall, sagging grasses. A marsh hen's call rose, warbling and chattering, over the morning stillness. It was a warm, fresh, crisp morning—and I hope you understand what I mean by "crisp." It almost felt like the whole world had been born anew and was just beginning to take its first breath.

Suddenly, I was jolted out of my pensive state by a noisy truck pulling up by the marsh's shore, near where Aunt Emma's car was parked. The rattling truck was pulling a large trailer that held six kayaks, all brightly colored, and an array of life jackets and paddles. Stepping out of his truck, the tour guide greeted us. He was a tall, blond young man of around twenty.

"Hello, folks!" he greeted us, clasping his hands together. "Looks like perfect kayaking weather! The other two members of our tour should be here in a minute, so you can go ahead and choose your kayak."

Connor immediately selected a bright orange one—his favorite color. Aunt Emma chose a long, blue kayak with a streak of yellow down its side. I took longer determining which one I would paddle through the marsh, and finally decided on a deep reddish-yellow one, the color of a Saint Simons sunset. It looked sturdy and had a storage compartment which would hold my camera and water bottle.

I checked my watch. It was already 8:13. I wondered where the other two kayakers were and why they hadn't arrived yet. The guide seemed to have read my thoughts.

"The others just booked their trip yesterday. It was pretty short notice, but they said it was important—I guess they couldn't make it to any other tours this week," he informed me. Connor and I were beginning to grow restless when, finally, the other members of our tour drove up. They parked their black Honda right beside Aunt Emma's green Bug. I smiled, and walked toward where Aunt Emma and the guide were standing. We were finally about to be off!

My exuberance was suddenly cut short when the other two tour members stepped out of their car. No—my exuberance wasn't cut short. It was more like abruptly and immediately ended. My stomach seemed to sink to my toes. I closed my eyes, and opened them, hoping this was simply some bad dream and that I would wake up. However, nothing could change the fact that there, standing right in front of me, were Winston and Ben.

I tried to appear cool and calm, but Connor, standing beside me, did nothing to hide his surprised look. Pinching his arm, I turned around to take the paddle the guide was handing me.

The guide—who introduced himself as Ian—began to instruct us in the proper way to paddle. That was all old information for me. Barely paying attention to what Ian was saying, I eyed Winston suspiciously. He didn't make eye contact with me. Instead, he simply stood there, swiping his paddle through the air as instructed.

I didn't know what Winston was up to, but I determined to keep my eyes open for clues. Things were starting to get really interesting, and Connor and I both knew it.

Chapter Six:
High Tides

The wind was blowing only mildly as we set off, providing a gentle breeze. The salty water, framed by miles of marsh grasses, was home to all manner of sea life, including dolphins — my favorite marine animal. Ian pointed out many of the various species of birds native to this part of The Island as we paddled through the rivers and outlets of the marsh.

"The water level changes with the tides," Ian informed us. "It's close to high tide now, but at low tide, none of these little channels are here. In fact, the water level often reaches the muck at the bottom of the marsh."

"So that's why we have to kayak so early?" I questioned.

"Exactly right!" Ian said. "We certainly wouldn't want to get stuck in the muck, would we? And also, there are oyster beds at the bottom of the marsh, which you could cut yourself on. It can be dangerous for kayakers at low tide." He looked around. "Any questions?"

"Yes," Aunt Emma paddled her kayak alongside his. "How would you distinguish between the different species of..." Aunt Emma, an avid bird-watcher and a nature enthusiast, had finally found a kindred spirit with all the answers to her numerous questions. I slowed my pace and waited for Connor to catch up. He paddled so close I thought our kayaks would collide.

"Heard anything suspicious yet?" I asked. "I presumed you were spying on them, since it took you so long to catch up."

Connor rolled his eyes. "Very funny, Ethan."

"Sorry, I'm just kidding. Kayaking can be difficult for first-timers, I suppose...especially the steering," I stopped, lowering my voice. "But in a sense, I'm not kidding. Winston is watching our every move. I think it's time we watched his. Could you help me just this once?" Connor splashed some water at my face.

"Ethan, forget it! I already told you—I was nice once, and I helped you. But I don't want to get involved in this operation. It's—well, it could be dangerous! I don't want to be a spy. I came here for vacation, and I plan to keep it that way." He paddled swiftly and silently toward Ian and Aunt Emma, who were now quite a little way ahead of us, the ripples from their strokes shifting back in long intervals. I barely noticed Winston's presence until he was right beside me.

"Hey, kid," he whispered. "You look familiar. Oh...you were at the lighthouse when I was doing my inspection."

"Yes, I remember you." I said bluntly, then continued boldly. "If I recall, you were trying to determine the logistics of breaking into the lighthouse and stealing the Fresnel lens."

"Stealing the lens?" he said, pausing for a long moment, as if thinking something over. "I...I don't know what you mean."

"Oh, really?" I replied. "Then why were you stalking us all the way to Fort Frederica?"

"Kid, you know that whole incident was a coincidence. Come on."

"Yeah, right," I retorted, trying to figure out

Winston's game. He was trying to fool me, but I had already seen too much. "You're not going to do anything to the lighthouse. So just stop stalking me. You can't follow me everywhere."

"Is all that so?" he asked. "Where will you be going tomorrow, then?" I didn't answer. He added, "What if I already know?"

I was silent. I wasn't going to let his ridiculous questions scare me. He chuckled to himself, and I paddled away from him, past Connor, until I was alongside Aunt Emma's blue kayak. She and Ian were still chatting as she snapped pictures of the many birds which chirped within the grasses.

"These will go wonderfully in my wildlife scrapbook!" she exclaimed. I stopped paddling for a minute, letting Aunt Emma and the guide paddle ahead of me. I glanced over my shoulder. Connor was paddling at a slow pace, with Winston and Ben behind him in their kayaks, following on either side. They were talking quietly. Sighing, I kept paddling as I was. I felt stuck in the middle, both in our kayaking trip and in life. I had three choices of what to do: I could tell Aunt Emma and end the whole thing, I could silently end it and tell only Connor, or I could continue trying to stop this mysterious lighthouse theft. I simply couldn't decide between what was wiser and what could lead to adventure. Above all, I really wanted to keep the lighthouse safe—to guard it if I could.

I looked behind me. There were three kayaks and three people. I turned back around and kept paddling. For a minute or two I paddled in peace, enjoying the beauty of God's creation. From all around came the voices of different marsh birds, and behind I heard many splashes as each of our paddles dug into the water.

Suddenly, I heard a huge splash from behind me, as if something had suddenly hit the water with a smack. A few droplets hit the back of my neck.

I looked behind me. There were three kayaks but two people. I turned my kayak around and paddled toward Winston and Ben.

"Where's Connor?" I demanded. Winston gave me an evil smile.

"You had better hope your cousin can swim!" he laughed. "Ben, I'll paddle ahead and get some 'help.' You know what I mean." Ben nodded, and Winston paddled quickly up the stream.

Suddenly I caught sight of Connor flailing his arms several yards off—fortunately, wearing a life jacket. I glared violently at Ben. He only smiled threateningly back at me. Impulsively, I thrust myself out of the kayak and, grabbing my paddle, slipped quickly into the water. Thankfully, it was July, so the water wasn't cold. I gripped my paddle and swam toward where Connor was hopelessly thrashing about. Gripping his arm, I glanced behind me. My kayak had begun to float away, toward Winston, Aunt Emma, and Ian. Ben hurried after it.

Although I was an excellent swimmer, it didn't seem that Connor had ever swum in his life. His life jacket and my arm were his only support. I tried to speak some sense into Connor, but he insisted on being hysterical. Up ahead, it seemed that Ben was rummaging through my kayak. Winston, feigning concern, paddled quickly and called out for help from Ian.

Afraid of the sharp oyster beds which lay beneath my feet, I leaned backwards and instructed Connor to do the same. Ian and Aunt Emma, realizing our peril, whirled their kayaks around and rowed toward us rapidly, with Winston following at their backs. I was already assisting Connor as he climbed back into his kayak, steadying the orange craft.

Ian finally arrived, helping me to slip back into my own kayak.

"Are you all right?" Ian asked. Connor and I nodded. "That's good," he continued, "But what happened?"

"Um...well," Connor began.

"Connor tipped, and I jumped out to get him. No problem," I stated quickly. Ian seemed mostly convinced by my explanation.

"Okay," Ian said, "Are you sure you're all right?" Connor nodded a second time. "Well, I guess that we'll continue our voyage. Right this way, folks." And he paddled off.

The peaceful, halcyon waters, disturbed only by the twelve paddles that tore smoothly through them, brought to my memory the poetry of Sidney Lanier — the great Georgian poet who described these very waterlands in his poem "The Marshes of Glynn":

As the marsh-hen secretly builds on the watery sod,

Behold I will build me a nest on the greatness of God:

I will fly in the greatness of God as the marsh-hen flies

In the freedom that fills all the space 'twixt the
marsh and the skies:

By so many roots as the marsh-grass sends in the
sod

I will heartily lay me a-hold on the greatness of
God:

Oh, like to the greatness of God is the greatness
within

The range of the marshes, the liberal marshes of
Glynn.

Mom was especially fond of that poem.

My thoughts were drawn back to the present as I
saw we were coming to the end of our tour. As I
propelled myself through the water, I began to consider
two things. First, that Connor needed some serious
swimming lessons. But second, why would Winston try
to get Connor to capsize? What purpose did he have
doing it? I was so lost in thought that I wasn't even
watching where my kayak was going. Suddenly, I
found myself in the midst of the marsh grasses, which
was not so bad until — sand flies! They were all around
me: in my face, on my kayak, and everywhere! As I
pushed myself hastily out of the grass, I heard
snickering behind me. Connor was laughing so hard,
his boat was wobbling.

Serves him right if he tips again, I thought wryly

while I splashed water on myself to ward off the flies. As we neared the shore, I shifted my position in the kayak and heard the sound of crumpling paper. I looked into my kayak, and there, on my seat, was a water-stained, slightly crumpled piece of paper. I slid it into my pocket and stopped my kayak from skidding on the stones at the shore, for we were back at our starting point.

"Sorry that you tipped. It happens to a lot of...first timers." Ian the tour guide grinned. Connor glowered back at him.

Winston shook his head. "Thank you for the trip, sir. We've had lots of fun..." His voice trailed off, giving way to a hideous grin.

"Okay...that's just great. I'm glad you enjoyed the trip," Ian said slowly, unsettled by Winston's eerie presence. The two thieves in disguise walked to their car, and we marched over to ours. I rode all the way home in suspense, the piece of paper practically burning a hole in my pocket. I dared not open it with Aunt Emma sitting right beside me. What was it, and why had Winston staged the whole thing simply to give it to me?

Once at home, I unfolded the wrinkled scrap of paper and read it.

> Don't try to stop us
> Or "save" the lighthouse and lens
> Else you'll be sorry
>
> Surely wouldn't want
> Anything else to happen
> To both of you kids

It was perfect haiku stanzas. However, it was more than that. It was a threat, and it was a little bit frightening, for it was a promise that something bad might to happen to me. Perhaps Connor was right.

Maybe I should give up...but no, I couldn't! Then, I realized something else was with the poem—another piece of paper, stuck to the haiku by water. Had Ben dropped it by accident?

In quickly scribbled print, the paper read:

Ben,
THIS IS IMPORTANT. Under real necessity, every talented thief enjoys lightly implying greed, hate— toying long, even voraciously, about nearer subjects that, oddly, rarely yield to hard enterprises. Every nitpicky design offers fantastic botherations of terrible heaviness. Bored of older, kneeling stupidities, this head entertained ridiculous enterprises. Inside, secretive attacks collapsed lifeless under evil things, hastily attracting the inner secrets, masked. Yearning purposefully under ridiculous purpose, old structure enters into territory inside severed intentions. Now things have eminent links. Inside, great havens— thoughts—hold over, under, seeing everything. I HAVE THOUGHT MUCH, AND THIS WILL HAPPEN.

IN CLOSING,
WINSTON

This was most definitely a clue. I gazed at it intently, but very little of it made sense. It seemed particularly covert—as if it was hiding something terrible. Winston probably didn't want me to have this piece of information, but I had it anyway.

Things were getting really interesting.

Chapter Seven:
Old Enough For Fairy Tales

After I rescued him, Connor became quite a bit more amiable toward me. He was now officially "in" — my detective partner in our new-found mystery. After all, I had just proved to him reason #2, about the great water sports and beaches (although capsizing wasn't part of the reasons). It felt great for him to be so much more open-minded, and I felt that I really, really could prove all the reasons to him. Well, at least I *hoped* I could...

Later that night, Connor, Aunt Emma, and I all sat in the living room of my house. Everything was serene and quiet. Outside, I saw dim silhouettes of live oaks and their Spanish moss in the evening moonlight. Aunt Emma cleared her throat, continuing to read a home design magazine. Connor, too, was absorbed in a book — my well-worn copy of *The Hobbit*. I smiled. From the look on his face, he was no longer sitting in my living room; he was walking the mountains and forests of Middle-Earth. Good fiction always does that same thing to me. It pulls me out of my world for a little while, then puts me back as a better person. I glanced down at my book of choice — *The Horse and His Boy* by C.S. Lewis — and I had the sudden, fleeting realization that I was reading a children's book. Then I remembered something Lewis himself once said: "Some day you will be old enough to start reading fairy tales again." In actuality, I had never grown out of Lewis's stories of Narnia in the first place.

After reading a couple chapters, I closed the

book and relaxed in the recliner. Summer had flopped on the floor next to me. I remembered when we first got her—that little golden, spunky Labradoodle puppy—four years ago in July. It had been one of the hottest summers I had known in Saint Simons; thus, my dad proposed to name her Summer.

As I closed my tired eyes for a moment, I felt a buzz in my pocket. Pulling out my phone, I saw there was one new message—one new message from my cousin Cassidy. I viewed the text:

How's my favorite oldest cousin on my mother's side, once removed?

Then another:

Well not once removed. ;)

I smiled and texted back:

I'm great! But, you forgot your comma after the word "well."

Grammar geek! :P It's summer now. No more school. Period.

I smiled again.

Okay, deal. No more grammar corrections.

Cassidy promptly responded,

Thank you.

I paused for a moment. Should I tell Cassidy about the mysterious happenings at the lighthouse? She was sort of like a sister...perhaps she ought to know. I jotted out a text, but hesitated in sending it. My finger waited over the "send" button. I had almost convinced myself not to send it when hands grabbed my shoulders from behind. I started, and my finger bumped "send." Connor laughed, and I turned my head and glared at him humorously.

"Who ya texting?" he asked, peering over my shoulder. "Your girlfriend?"

I rolled my eyes. "No, my cousin on the other side of the family. Cassidy."

"Oh," he said. "And?"

"And" I replied slowly, "she now knows about what's going on. With you-know-what and you-know-who." Connor didn't look surprised; he just looked pleased.

"Sounds good," he said and turned to leave.

Cassidy and I chatted for a little longer. She was thrilled about the whole mystery, and vowed to help when and if I needed her. I couldn't help but feel that, eventually, we just might need her bubbly enthusiasm in this escapade.

As Connor and I were walking up the stairs going to bed that night, a sudden shock of realization hit me. I had been wondering how Winston and Ben had been tracking our every move, but up until now, I hadn't known how. However, I had now figured it out!

"Eureka!" I said aloud, causing Connor to jump. He turned to me with a face of concern.

"Ethan...are you all right?" he asked, one eyebrow raised.

"Oh, yes! I'm more than fine — I'm great!" I leapt up the last two steps. "I've just figured out how Winston and Ben have been following us!"

"How?" he questioned, both eyebrows now raised.

"You know the list I showed you the first day you were here?" I asked. He nodded slowly. "Well, my copy was the schedule of all the things we were going to do. It even had the dates and the times we wanted to do them!"

"Where are you going with this, Ethan?" Connor asked.

"Don't you see? The day we saw the lighthouse, I sat on a bench in the lobby while you and Aunt Emma used the restroom. I never saw the list after that! It must have fallen out when we set my backpack on the bench..."

"...and Winston picked it up!" Connor finished excitedly.

"Bingo!" I confirmed. "So he knows everything we did, and everything we are going to do."

"Wow, smarty! Someone needs to zip their backpack shut, so they don't get in trouble, huh?" Connor teased.

"Oh yeah?" I shot back playfully. "Someone needs to zip their mouth shut, so they don't get in trouble, eh?"

Connor laughed sarcastically. "We're visiting the historic Christ Church for the Sunday service tomorrow, right?" Connor asked.

"Yep," I replied. "And I'd expect to see Winston, and maybe even Ben, there."

Chapter Eight:
Thou Shalt Not Steal

We arrived in the Christ Church parking lot at eleven o'clock sharp on the third of July. Christ Church was one of the oldest churches in all of Georgia, and it was simply brimming with historical treasure. Aged oaks dangled their branches around its walls and steeple. Aunt Emma decided it would be a great vacation highlight for Connor, since we could go to church and see a historic landmark all in one.

The white, steepled church was enthroned in history. In 1884, a man named Anson Dodge oversaw the building of the church by workers from his father's sawmill. As some of these workers were former shipbuilders, they assembled the parish building in a similar fashion, seamlessly constructing the building in the shape of a cross. The pure white of the church contrasted with the vivid green grass spreading across the lawn under the trees' canopy.

An usher greeted us at the door, and then we shuffled quietly to one of the old, sturdy wooden benches which lined the walls on either side. It was amazing to realize the rich history of the building and think about the people who had worshipped and were buried there. I glanced up and down the aisle, and, sure enough, there was Winston, his tall figure protruding from above the pew. He was sitting on the opposite side from us, about two rows back.

The priest, a clean-shaven man with a friendly smile, stepped behind the pulpit and cleared his throat. He had a bold, neighborly voice, and the sound of his words echoed throughout the room. The usual prayers, songs, and Scripture readings were offered, and then the priest began his sermon.

"This week, I'm going to discuss the eighth commandment and its practical aspects," he began. "The eighth commandment, as stated in chapter twenty of the book of Exodus, says, 'Thou shalt not steal.' This important command is significant and can show us how to better treat others."

I glanced back at Winston. He was shifting uncomfortably in his seat. I suppose the words, "Thou shalt not steal" were echoing in his mind. I stifled an oncoming giggle.

The priest continued, "Stealing is abominable. Whether a small or valuable item, it is wrong. We all know this to be wrong. However, often we simply *wish* to steal. This is called coveting, and it is discussed later in this same chapter. Planning to steal or simply coveting in your heart, is just as bad as the act of thieving itself. The Bible says, 'Be on your guard against all covetousness, for one's life does not consist in the abundance of his possessions.'"

I glanced back at Winston, flashing him a triumphant smirk. He only glared. He couldn't wait for the sermon to be over. I actually found the sermon quite interesting and helpful, though *somebody* obviously didn't.

The priest concluded, "So be careful, whether coveting an item, stealing in secret, or even giving in to discontentment, for God sees the hearts of men. Rarely does anyone get away with thievery. Christ is a righteous judge, though He is also merciful," he finished. I didn't bother to look back at Winston. I knew that he was probably squirming in his seat, just yearning for church to be over.

After church was dismissed, Aunt Emma hung around inside for a bit, chatting with the other churchgoers. Connor and I slipped out, telling her we would be waiting for her in the car. She waved us away with her hand and continued talking. I smiled at Connor. This was working out just perfectly.

"Now—to our plan!" I whispered as we exited the building and trotted down the sidewalk. Winston was wishing to get out, but had gotten stuck in the dense crowd at the back of the church. That was great, for if he was gone, our counterattack plan would crash.

We crossed the street to the parking lot. Besides all the cars, the lot was practically deserted of people. Connor and I scurried across the street toward the old, dented, black Honda which was parked peculiarly close to Aunt Emma's lime Bug, only three spaces down. I knew Winston wanted to be as close as he could get to us. I grabbed out my notebook and pen as we reached his car.

"Ready, Ethan?" Connor asked.

"Yes," I replied. "He left us a haiku note, so I suppose we'll just leave him one!" I began to tear out the sheet of paper that I had transcribed last night, containing a perfect haiku on it.

"He's really going to beat himself up for letting us get this close to his car," Connor commented.

"Nope, not this time, boys!" a voice from behind us startled me and sent my heart momentarily pounding out of my chest. I spun around, nearly knocking Connor over. There was Ben. Although he was only of an average height, he wasn't the sort you wanted to face alone—he looked strong and solidly built. However, I pushed those thoughts aside. I *wasn't* alone—I had Connor. Connor was my companion now; he was my friend. I took a deep breath.

"Hello, Ben," I said. "Did you enjoy the kayak tour yesterday?" I asked casually.

"Quit playing around, kiddo," he snapped. "Oh, and in fact, I did enjoy the tour yesterday."

"Really," Connor stepped into the conversation with a sly grin. "You seemed to be paddling a bit slow, you nincompoop!" I rolled my eyes at Connor's silliness.

"Nincompoop? You're just a stupid kid!" Ben retorted, raising a muscular arm.

"I'm fourteen years old, thank you very much!" Connor shot back with equal enthusiasm. In this conversation with Ben, Connor truly surprised me. I was beginning to see a more bold, daring side of my seemingly quiet cousin.

Ben looked at Connor, snorted, and glared. "Oh, whatever. I'll just cut to the chase. Winston has a message for you two: quit trying to meddle around with us, or there will be trouble! We're smarter than you think."

"Oh yeah? That message wasn't half so catchy as his previous note." Connor began, when I grabbed his arm.

"Connor, just quit! Winston has just come out, and Aunt Emma's near the doorway!" I pulled him toward the car. However, Ben wasn't done talking.

"Don't forget! If you keep at this game, Winston will have you in checkmate before you can say 'rook.' Am I clear?" he demanded.

"I don't even know how to play chess!" Connor retorted. Ben jumped in the car and cranked it, quickly swerving back onto the road and pausing to pick up Winston.

I turned to look at the church. Aunt Emma, finally finishing her goodbyes, was striding our way. We hurriedly stood by the Bug, trying to appear aimless and impatient.

"Boys!" she called. "Why aren't you in the car?"

"Um..." I faltered. "It was...locked."

"Oh," she pressed the unlock button on her key-remote. "Hop in, boys! Lunchtime!"

We both entered the car as Aunt Emma started the engine. I took the front seat this time and left Connor to the back. Connor texted me: *What on earth was Ben talking about? U know, all that game and rook stuff? Like I said, I don't even know how to play chess.*

I laughed quietly, my mind already on a delicious lunch of fried shrimp at Jinright's in Brunswick. I wrote back: *Well, then, it's a good thing I do.*

Chapter Nine:
Fishing for Clues

That night, Aunt Emma decided to take us for a picnic dinner on the beach. We arrived around six p.m., finding the beach fairly crowded, but bearable. After all, it was July, and a big Island holiday also. We began spreading out a beach towel for a picnic blanket.

"You two boys go swim and hang out. I'll fix the picnic," she motioned toward the gentle waves crashing against the shore. The pier stretched out into the ocean, hovering above the waters; and beyond that was the Sidney Lanier Bridge, which led from Brunswick to nearby Jekyll Island.

"Thanks, Aunt Emma," I said, turning around. Connor was already in the water. I dashed across the sand to join him. I waded out, deeper and deeper as the water seemed to cleanse me with its salty bath of rolling waves. When the water grew too deep for me to stand, I closed my eyes and floated along. This was just another reason why I loved The Island. I felt as if I must have been born a fish—not that I was an expert swimmer, but I had taken to the saltwater my whole life. I loved sand. I loved water. I loved the smell of salty air and the sound of seagulls cooing. This was me.

I saw Connor standing several yards off, his slim form remaining still as the waves crashed against his ankles. After paddling a bit, I stood up and strode over to him, grinning. Connor did not seem to be used to enjoying the beach so much. Though he was probably having a wonderful time, I thought he looked like a polar bear that was stuck in the Bahamas.

"Having fun?" I questioned.

"Oh, yes," he replied. I silently scooped my hand underwater, looking for the spots of underwater mud, and formed a ball of sandy muck. While Connor's back was turned, I hurled it at him. He spun around to see me grabbing my stomach in laughter. However, when I looked up, a muck-ball was launching toward me. I ducked underwater, the mud barely hitting my head and running down my cheeks. Connor, in turn, laughed good-naturedly.

"You're crazy, you know that?" Connor asked.

"Of course," I laughed, crossing my eyes and giving him an absurd face. I was preparing another muck ball when we saw Aunt Emma motioning us up for our picnic. We both walked back across the sandy beach, being careful not to step on any oblivious tourists or carefully crafted sandcastles.

The supper was delicious—chicken salad sandwiches with Cokes—and we ate quickly. I glanced around the beach. Many people that I had known didn't like St. Simons as well as some beaches; they complained that the water wasn't blue enough, or the sand wasn't soft enough, or any number of things. Nevertheless, I knew that I loved it more than any other place in the world, although I couldn't quite put it into words...

"What would you like to do now, boys?" Aunt Emma asked as we finished the picnic. She wiped her mouth carefully. "Shall we stay here, or go shop in the Village?"

I cut in before Connor could. "It's time Connor went to the Village, don't you think? Let's go...I'll carry the picnic basket." We cleaned up our things, and threw on t-shirts and flip-flops; I grabbed the basket and began skipping toward the car, humming a happy tune. I can't say I was whistling a tune, because I wasn't. I never have figured out how to whistle; I suppose it's just one of those things that only comes to some people.

I was happy because the Village would most definitely get Connor one step closer to believing me and believing my reasons, and...well, in the back of my mind, I thought I could get some detective work done. Perhaps there would be clues.

I thought of this as we walked to the car.

The Village is an area right near the Saint Simons pier & lighthouse. It is a place with lots of small, locally owned restaurants and stores with a brilliant ocean view not far away. Parallel rows of shops sporting their various wares stretch far down the street. As I had expected, the Village was crowded. After all, it was Fourth of July weekend, and tourists had streamed into The Island for this long-expected annual holiday.

As we slipped into a souvenir store, I glanced over my shoulder. The beach's horizon, which was within view over the edge of Mallery Street, shone with the beginnings of a gorgeous, glistening sunset. The deep, reddish-orange rays seemed to reach down, through the sky, through the streets, and — in a way — into the heart of every islander. Accompanying the sunset's magnificence was the lighthouse's swiveling lens, which sent a bright beam around the pier. However, even the lighthouse looked dim and dingy in the crimson brilliance of the setting sun. The sky above The Island was like God's canvas, painted with skill and beauty.

By the time we finished browsing through the shop, the once red-orange sky now held hues of deep magenta. I was enjoying myself so much that I realized something startling—I hadn't even been looking for Winston and Ben! They could have been tracking us the whole evening, and I would have known nothing of it! I determined from then onward to keep my eyes open.

As Aunt Emma and Connor walked into a clothing store, I informed Aunt Emma that I was going to sit on a bench outside the shop's front door. She nodded at me, then immediately began examining a lavender blouse.

I parked myself on the long, wooden bench and rubbed my forehead. I simply needed to clear my head, which was currently swimming with too much information, too many worries, and too many thoughts to take in. I began sorting my thoughts.

- I've potentially proved three reasons to Connor—a big change from the beginning!
- We think we know something of what Winston and Ben are doing, but not how they are going to do it.
- Tomorrow is the Fourth of July—the date of the intended robbery!
- No one else knows but me and Connor—and Cassidy.

I now felt much better, and yet much worse. Part of me just wanted to give in, tell the grown-ups, and end the whole thing. But should I? They might just pass us off as making up outlandish tales and reading too much into things. Wasn't this the fun of a mystery, doing things on your own? I struggled with myself. I knew I might have been making the wrong choice, but what could I do?

And that nonsense note Ben had accidentally dropped...was it important? Was it a clue?

Suddenly, I noticed two people at the street's corner, standing and talking to each other. One was a tall, attractive young lady — seemingly in her mid-twenties — with deep brown hair and a charming smile. The other was a dark-haired, long-nosed, string bean of a human wearing a most convincingly dashing grin. He was Winston.

I realized that if he saw me, especially if Aunt Emma saw him see me, things could get very ugly very quickly. So I pulled from my backpack a pair of sunglasses and a baseball cap, which I promptly put on. I scooted to the far side of the bench, intent on hearing their conversation.

Winston was speaking, "The beauty of the sunset pales in comparison to yours."

"Oh, Winston," the woman laughed, brushing a lock of hair behind her head, "You always were too poetic! Just tell me what you really think." I sniggered at Winston's flowery dialogue. Winston — in love! It simply couldn't be. He was likely up to something. Then he spoke again.

"Julia, I — um — greatly enjoy your company," he said with a false flourish. "It would be wonderful if we met here tomorrow, to see the fireworks together. What do you think?"

Julia responded, "Oh, yes, let's meet at the lighthouse gift shop, if that's okay. I'll be done with all my work there and also with my errands by six." Winston nodded at her. "Okay. I plan to see you then."

"Goodbye then, Julia," he said. Julia walked toward her car, but Winston lingered for a moment. Suddenly his phone rang. Answering, he said, "Hello, Ben? Thanks for calling back...yes, I did. She totally fell for it...what? No...no...of course not. Look, Ben...those two teenagers are not a problem. I've totally got them off our scent. They think it's all about the lighthouse and the lens...wait a sec. I gotta go." There was a reason Winston had to go so quickly. He had noticed a familiar-looking teenage guy sitting on a bench. He had eyed the young fellow, and edged subtly closer to him. And then the guy had gotten up and swiftly entered a store.

That guy was me, of course.

I entered the nearest store—a different one than Aunt Emma and Connor were in—and glanced over my shoulder, looking for a place to hide. I strode to the back of the shop, trying not to look suspicious. Winston entered the store slowly, peering around. I ducked behind a rack of clothing. Winston walked around a corner into another section of the store and I rushed out as quickly as I could without appearing suspect.

I imagined how it would feel to be invisible, blending in seamlessly with the asphalt below my feet, still cooling from the day's heat. There certainly are times when being invisible would be convenient.

Striding across the road, I hurried toward the shadows of a store which had already closed for the evening. The darkness behind the store helped conceal me. I spotted a police car parked a block away—some comfort in that. Then Winston emerged from the store, glancing about in all directions. I pulled my peering face back into the shadows and held my breath. Winston took another scan of the premises, checked his watch, and strode off to his car. I waited until he was gone to move.

When I had barely made it back across the street, Aunt Emma and Connor exited the store they were in, each with a bag in hand.

"Ethan, look! I got this awesome 'SSI' shirt for a souvenir! It's so..." he stopped suddenly. "Are you all right?"

I nodded. "I'm fine." I had the feeling Connor was getting used to this—every time I was left alone, I always had more evidence to tell him. I could see from the look on his face that he realized I knew something he didn't—and he had to find out.

As we passed the many storefronts, I glanced over my shoulder. I saw no sign of Winston. What Winston had said shocked me: had he had been purposefully leading me off his trail? If so, then what was this mystery all about? I felt as if I were fishing for clues, yet catching rather little. Since tomorrow was the Fourth, I knew I had to catch something bigger—and soon! My mind suddenly turned again to the strange note that had been accidentally dropped into my kayak. Somehow, I knew the answer lay there.

Chapter Ten:
End of the Pier

The shops of the Village stretched on for a while, nearly to the end of Mallery Street. Yet once the street ended, there was even more to see along the edge of the pier.

Walking along the covered walkway which ran above the beach, over the waves, and into an open-air balcony, we made our way to the end of the Saint Simons Pier. From here one could always get a fantastic view of the southern tip of The Island and of the lighthouse, standing tall like a giant candlestick in the night.

And that got me thinking. I thought of all the wonderful evenings I had spent here, by the pier. Chief in my mind were the memories of the Fourth of July holiday. When the sun went down and the fireworks began, the whole island was in for a spectacular show. My family always came and set up chairs in the middle of the road amidst the celebrating islanders. When we were young, my cousin Cassidy and I always waited expectantly for the fireworks as if they were Christmas Day itself. We would gaze at the different colors and explosions that lit up the sky. *Would this Fourth of July be different?* I pondered, almost sadly.

I decided it was time to give everyone a good laugh—something I seemed to do often, even if I wasn't trying. Striding to the right walkway which branched out from the main one, I walked to the very edge over the water and stood facing Aunt Emma and Connor, who stood yards away.

"Hey, Connor!" I shouted. "Watch."

And then I jumped backward off the edge.

Connor came running, incredulous that I had jumped into the water, and Aunt Emma followed behind, chuckling softly. When Connor reached the edge, he saw the last thing he expected — me, crouching on a lower platform. He narrowed his eyes as I laughed loudly.

"Sorry," I grinned, "I couldn't resist. It fools everyone."

He snickered slightly. "It's okay. That is pretty funny."

The dim lights along the pier made curious reflections in the murky water along the shore. Further down the coast, the sea cast her deep, blue breakers against the sand and rocks. The lighthouse still shone, its bright beam revolving in the calm night.

I sat at the kitchen table, Winston's note to Ben lying in front of me. My head was in my hands, and my fingers ran through my tousled brown hair. Clicking a button on my phone, I checked the time on its illuminated screen. 10:37 p.m.

I groaned, and continued staring at the paper. It was an enigma that had my brain in knots. I stared at the confusing text:

Ben,

THIS IS IMPORTANT. Under real necessity, every talented thief enjoys lightly implying greed, hate — toying long, even voraciously, about nearer subjects that, oddly, rarely yield to hard enterprises. Every nitpicky design offers fantastic botherations of terrible heaviness. Bored of older, kneeling stupidities, this head entertained ridiculous enterprises. Inside, secretive attacks collapsed lifeless under evil things, hastily attracting the inner secrets, masked. Yearning purposefully under ridiculous purpose, old structure enters into territory inside severed intentions. Now things have eminent links. Inside, great havens— thoughts—hold over, under, seeing everything. I HAVE THOUGHT MUCH, AND THIS WILL HAPPEN.

IN CLOSING,
WINSTON

I couldn't make out its meaning. Obviously, he was talking about his secret plans. "Old structure"— that seemed to refer to the lighthouse. But what about the sentences in all capitals? Perhaps he was signifying an important point? Some of it just sounded like nonsense: "toying long," "fantastic botherations," "severed intentions."

It was getting late. The more I thought about the note, the more confused I felt. It simply did not make sense to my brain.

Hearing Aunt Emma softly snoring on the couch, I looked up. Connor had risen out of his chair in the living room and was walking toward the kitchen table where I sat befuddled. A sleepy smile was on his face.

"Whatcha working on?" he asked quietly.

"Come see," I said, my voice pale and tired. "To be honest, I'm not exactly sure." Connor sat down beside me and squinted at the paper. He mouthed something silently, his eyes darting across the page.

"What do you think?" I questioned. He held up his hand for me to be quiet. His brow furrowed.

"I think I'm on to something," he said. "I'm thinking this note isn't quite what it seems." He looked me in the eyes. "It's a cipher."

"A secret message," I whispered. "Of course." *Why didn't I think of that?* I thought.

Connor and I were examining every word on the page, trying to make sense of it—and trying to find the coded message that was probably hidden there. Connor also was puzzled.

"I studied a tiny bit about codes and ciphers in school once. But this all makes sense. It's real sentences, not jumbled-up nonsense."

"Yet it doesn't really make much sense," I pointed out. "He doesn't seem to be making any real point. That's why I am sure you're right. This has to be a coded message."

Suddenly we heard Aunt Emma yawning. I grabbed the note, hastily folded it up, and stuffed it in my pocket. Aunt Emma stood up slowly, and glanced over at us.

"Time for bed, boys," she said sleepily. "It's almost eleven."

I stood, acting tired. But inside, I wasn't thinking of rest or sleep.

I was waging a war—a war that hinged upon solving a cipher.

Chapter Eleven:
The Plan

Once safely alone upstairs, I was finally able to tell Connor all I had heard earlier in the Village. The close encounter with Winston, in particular, excited him. His eager ears gathered in everything I had to say.

After I finished, he remained silent for a moment. Then, looking me in the eye, he said, "You want to know something Ethan? This is kind of off-topic, but anyway...I really like the feel of this island. Tonight's shopping trip was awesome—all the people are so friendly and ready to help. All these local shops and restaurants...well, they're just great." He awaited my response.

I was slightly startled, not expecting such a reply. Raising my head, I said, "Connor, you just nearly quoted my third reason."

"I know," he stated casually, "And?"

I hesitated, not knowing what to say. Then, instead of responding, I faked a yawn. "Time to hit the hay! After all, tomorrow's the Fourth—the biggest day of the summer here in Saint Simons!"

"Okay," Connor said with a laugh, exiting the room, "See you in the morning!" His figure disappeared, then quickly reappeared in my doorway again.

"Ethan?" he asked.

"Yes, Connor?" I responded.

"You have to figure this mystery out by tomorrow. You know that, don't you?" he asked.

I nodded. "I do. Why...why do you care so

much?"

He shrugged, then left. I flipped the light off, then sank into my bed as my head swam with plans, ideas, and fragmented thoughts. My brain spun and twirled like a vortex with no end. The past days' events and memories rushed by in a moment. I grappled aimlessly with words from Winston's note to Ben: *"Now things have eminent links. Inside, great havens — thoughts — hold over, under, seeing everything."*

Suddenly I sat bolt upright in bed. I had just experienced another one of those "eureka" moments. Tomorrow was coming soon, and I was ready for it — I hoped.

The next morning, we went over my plan, which was fantastic. Well, at least I thought so. Connor wasn't quite so easily convinced. Our major dispute revolved around one thing — involving the adults. I had relented to myself enough to let them into the plan, but Connor, now that he was involved, was adamantly against it.

"Why get the adults involved, Ethan?" he whined. "It makes it no fun, and they probably won't believe us!"

"Yeah, of course," I shot back, "And if we don't get their help, it makes it impossible. Get real, Connor. Adults rule the world. Adults are our key to solving this, to catching the thieves, and to ending this operation forever."

"Why?" Connor still persisted.

"Because," I replied, "If you think about it, adults have access to everything we need. They can get us to the pier, they can get us into the lighthouse, and they can catch Winston. It's our only chance. Plus, I'm four months older than you, and you have to do what I say."

Connor rolled his eyes. "I don't like it. But I guess you win."

I smiled slyly. "Okay, let's go over the plan again. First, we go to the museum and do a little research. I will explain all about Winston's note once we're there. Later, with backpacks full of proper equipment, we head to the pier early to set up chairs for the fireworks show. While Aunt Emma shops and stuff in the village, we get permission to take a walk down to the pier. Once there, we go back to the lighthouse museum area, where Julia and Winston are meeting. I believe Winston is using her to get into the lighthouse, but I haven't figured out exactly when yet. Anyway, then we wait for Winston to somehow get into the lighthouse—I don't know how he will do this—and then get the police. They're always around on the Fourth. When Winston walks down those 129 steps, he'll have a big surprise at the bottom."

"I guess it's okay, and we're only involving the police. After all, it'll still be us who solved the mystery," he affirmed. "But explain one thing now: tell me what you found out about the cipher."

"Well," I replied, "I was thinking about the last bit of the note: *'Now things have eminent links. Inside, great havens – thoughts – hold over, under, seeing everything.'* And that got me thinking about different kinds of secret codes. Sometimes codes just take single letters out of words, like the first letter or the last letter. So I spelled out that last sentence using the first letters of each word. You know what it spelled? 'N-T-H-E-L-I-

G-H-T-H-O-U-S-E.'"

"Huh." Connor was silent.

I continued. "So I wrote the whole thing out this morning. The capital words weren't part of the message—they were just capitalized to show that they were excluded from the cipher. The message reads: 'Burnette Lightle Vanstory. The end of both books. There is a clue. That is my purpose. It is in the lighthouse.' And a quick Internet search told me that Burnette Lightle Vanstory is an author of a few books about Saint Simons." That seemed to be explanation enough, for Connor was quiet a moment. Then he spoke.

"Ethan, I have to tell you something. The reason why I've never liked you is...well...you've always been so good at everything—school, sports, music, and stuff—and I sort of turned myself off to you. I..."

"I've done the exact same thing. You're not the only one at fault."

There was a long, awkward silence.

I thought of great stories where the heroes faced daunting impossibilities. Yet the impossibilities weren't truly impossible—they could be surmounted. Quests could be completed. Destinies could be fulfilled. However, the greatest difficulties were conquered with friends alongside.

"This whole thing seems too big for me," I thought aloud.

"We can do it...together. Really, it's exciting." Connor said with a smile. "But what do you think Aunt Emma will say when she finds out?"

"I don't know. Maybe—" I was cut off by Aunt Emma calling from downstairs.

"You boys start getting ready to go!" her voice hollered up.

"Yes, ma'am," I replied. "Be down in a minute." I smiled at Connor. "Time for step number one."

Chapter Twelve:
Gifts

I rushed down the stairs into the kitchen, but Aunt Emma wasn't there anymore. I glanced around, and then saw her sitting outside, in an ever-familiar bench swing. She watched, smiling, as Summer frolicked and played in the yard. Striding out of the house, I walked across the back porch and came to sit beside her on the swing. She was quiet for a long moment, staring into the distance. Then she spoke.

"It's so beautiful. What a gift!" she remarked.

"Gift?" I asked slowly.

"Ethan, all these trees, and the marsh, and the sand, and the blue sky—they're all gifts from God himself. It is His creation, after all," she told me, and then was again silent for a moment. "You know, I feel closer to God when I'm outside."

"Me too, Aunt Emma," I said, touching her hand, "Me too."

As we prepared to leave, my phone buzzed—a new message. I was surprised to see that it was from Mom: *How's your Fourth of July week going?*

I stood still for a moment. I had forgotten about Mom and Dad. She was probably on some mountain in Alaska now...or something like that. I imagined snow whipping around her, her hair blowing in the breeze. It seemed so strange—Alaska was such a far cry from the heat of south Georgia. What would mom think about all the odd goings-on? Before I even considered mentioning the lighthouse incidents, I hastily wrote back: *It's going great. Connor and I are getting along fine. :)*

Her response was brief: *Awesome! Dad and I love you and hope you enjoy yourself.*

I paused again, deep in thought. As I began to slip my phone into my pocket, I realized it wouldn't fit into the small hole. My wallet took up my left pocket, my iPod my right. Notebook, pen, and various papers were stuffed in the two other pockets of my cargo shorts.

I groaned, annoyed, then popped the bulky but protective case off my phone. It slid easily into my right pocket with my iPod, and I tossed the plastic case onto the kitchen countertop.

My Fourth of July adventure began with a trip to the Saint Simons Lighthouse gift shop. Connor and I were on a mission: find the books by this Burnette Lightle Vanstory, whom Winston had mentioned in his coded note to Ben. On any other day, we would have gone to the library. But since this was a holiday, the library was closed, so the lighthouse seemed to be the best place to start.

I browsed the gift shop, looking for any books under that name. The shop was full of knickknacks, jewelry, books, and other Saint Simons-related paraphernalia. However, I could find neither of the books, though both Connor and I scoured the store. If only the library was open! Without the books, this clue was utterly useless.

"It's no use. We may have to try somewhere else…" I whispered to Connor as we lingered in the rear of the gift shop. I had suddenly remembered that—during our Fort Frederica tour—I had seen in the gift shop a book by Burnette Vanstory. I shook my head and turned to Connor. "Obviously neither book is here. Either they don't sell them, or they're out of stock." Connor gave me an exasperated look.

"I should think that's obvious," he said straightforwardly. "If they don't have it, then...they don't have it." He grinned.

I smiled sardonically and poked him. But Connor was no longer looking at me.

"Look," Connor said, pointing. Then I turned around. And when I did, I almost gasped in surprise, because there was Julia, Winston's friend who worked at the lighthouse, with Winston right beside her. They stood in the doorway that led from the shop into the hallway. Connor and I ducked slightly and peered at them through some open shelves.

"All right," Julia was saying, "Then I will see you later here." Winston walked out the door, and Julia entered and greeted the woman working the cash register.

Then Connor had an idea which changed the day's course of events. It was so brilliant, and yet when he said it, it seemed so obvious. "Why don't we warn Julia and let her in on our plans?" I was startled. I looked at Julia, then back at Connor. He waited hesitantly for my response, knowing this would involve some major alterations to the plan. My plan.

"That is absolutely...crazy. But it's...smart. Really smart," I affirmed, knowing he was absolutely right. Connor smiled, looking pleased to finally have had a great idea before I did. Both our pairs of eyes traveled across the room. Julia, waving goodbye to the cash register worker, turned to leave the room. We followed her. Once in the cheery hall, Julia pulled out her smartphone, focusing intently on whatever she was typing.

Cautiously, I approached Julia. She looked up and smiled awkwardly.

"Hi," I said, not knowing where to start. Then, giving me the surprise of my life, Connor spoke up and explained our situation and Winston's lies. He briefly related all the happenings since that first visit to the lighthouse. Julia gasped when he was finished, trying to take in the whole situation.

"This must be some mistake," she said. "Winston wouldn't do this."

I shook my head vehemently. "No, it is no mistake! He's really doing this!" I pulled up a few pictures on my phone. "He's been stalking us for days, trying to stop us and get us off his trail."

"How horrible! How could...how could we stop him?" Julia asked, "Is there something you want me to do?"

"Um...yes, there is," I replied. "Do you know of an author named Burnette Lightle Vanstory? All I know is that he's an author, but I need some information on his books."

Julia laughed merrily, and I noticed her eyes sparkled with a deep, grayish blue. "First of all, Burnette Lightle Vanstory is not a him. She's a her. And secondly, yes, I do know of her. She was an amazing Saint Simons author, and one of my favorites."

"Was?" Connor asked.

"Yes, she died when she was nearly ninety-eight. But, fortunately, her legacy lives on in her books. They are treasures," Julia said. "The gift shop is out of them currently. I...I don't have any with me now...but...well..." she paused and seemed lost in thought. Her brow wrinkled with subtle lines of worry—even mistrust. "This all sounds a little unbelievable. Are you sure?"

"Positively," I replied, showing her more pictures, as well as the Burnette Vanstory clue. She bit a fingernail nervously, but the suspicion left her face.

"I can see you're right," she nodded, taking a deep breath. "And, as a matter of fact, I just remembered that I have a bag of books in the trunk of my car. I might—*might*—have those with me. I suppose we could go look."

I nodded. "That would be great, if you don't mind."

As we walked out the door toward Julia's little burgundy car, I noted Connor's excited face. He was like my partner—my lead general—my right-hand-man. I truly felt like Connor was my friend now. Our differences didn't matter. When you focus on your friend's differences and weaknesses, that is probably all you will see; but when you focus on your similarities and strengths, you will find yourselves true friends.

Chapter Thirteen: Meet Mrs. Vanstory

Once at her car, Julia popped open the trunk and pulled out a faded blue bag. She pulled a few titles out and set them aside, not finding the ones she wanted. I noted some of the books—both Saint Simons-related books like Eugenia Price's *Lighthouse*, and other books such as *Crime and Punishment*, *Moby Dick*, and one of my personal favorites, *The Lord of the Rings*. I could see that, although several books were about Saint Simons and the Golden Isles, they weren't the right ones. Finally, with a triumphant cry, she found one book and then the other.

She first handed me a thin, aged book. It was a navy blue hardcover, and its title was embossed in silver text. "Here is Mrs. Vanstory's first book. This one was written in 1950, back when she was Ms. Lightle. It's a small book, but it is a jewel." The book was titled, as I guessed by the clue, *Saint Simons Island*. Then she gave me the other title, *Georgia's Land of the Golden Isles*. "This was one of Mrs. Vanstory's later books. It's a history." I flipped through its pages, skimming the contents. It all looked fascinating, but I knew what I was really after—"the end of both books."

Julia's eyes widened suddenly, and she craned her neck as if hearing some deathly sound.

"Get behind the building. Now!" she hissed. I yanked Connor away, dashing behind the gift shop building in the nick of time, my heart quickening its pace. Of all people, Winston had just walked up. Rounding the corner, he stepped down the few stairs and came to stand by Julia's car.

Julia tried to hide her surprise and feigned a romantic attitude. "Oh, Winston! What a surprise. I thought you had left. What brings you back?"

Winston smiled. "Yes, indeed! I'm looking for a book — *Saint Simons Island* by Burnette Lightle. Do you have that one?" I gripped that very book tightly, barely breathing. My heart thudded in my chest. Connor and I stood with our backs up to the building, trying to listen to the conversation going on behind us.

"Um...no, I don't think I have it with me," Julia faltered slightly.

"Are you sure?" Winston pressed.

Back on the other side, we began to quietly investigate the two titles. Connor reached to grab the top book. I slapped his hand away. "Just a minute." I pulled the intercepted note from my pocket.

"The end is the answer to the mystery. It's a clue," I whispered. Without another word, I opened both books, finding the end pages of their main text. Surprisingly, both of the last lines were quotes from the Bible: "Ours is a goodly heritage" and "treasure that rust does not corrupt nor thieves break in and steal." I read these silently, then went over them in my head, puzzling over what this could mean. Obviously, Winston had been trying to tell Ben what he was after. What could it possibly be? I had heard from Winston's own mouth that his goal had nothing to do with the lens. So...what then? It was something else. I whispered these thoughts to Connor.

"Hmm," Connor thought. "Are you sure?"

"Yes, I'm sure. These clues from the two books seem to point to...treasure. Winston was trying to tell

Ben, through the secret message, that there was treasure hidden in the lighthouse."

Then Connor summed everything up in a way that made sense of it all. "He isn't after the lens, or even the lighthouse. But what he's after has to do with the lighthouse. He's looking for treasure, and the lighthouse is kind of like a treasure chest. Or so he thinks." His dark eyes danced with curiosity as he spoke.

I nodded. "We have to tell Julia, and find out what Winston is really after...before it's too late."

Meanwhile, I heard the voices growing nearer. I turned around and peeked for a brief moment around the corner. Their backs were turned, so I watched Winston's interaction with Julia closely.

"I know we used to be just friends...colleagues," Winston said, "But I always wanted something more. Tonight will be special. I'm looking forward to it." Julia looked genuinely flustered, but Winston obviously mistook it for mere bashfulness.

"Yes," she replied slowly, gazing into the distance, "Most wish for something more. Something beyond what their present, everyday life offers. It's the common theme in much literature: a quest for something greater, a longing for the impossible, a search for fulfillment." Winston nodded in agreement, and Julia continued after a brief hesitation. "But not everyone finds what they seek. The pure and the good characters usually find their heart's desires. Even the evil men sometimes find what they seek, but ultimately they are destroyed by guilt and pride."

Winston looked at her uncomfortably, almost suspiciously. She turned to him and met his eyes. "Don't you think so, friend?" she asked warmly.

Winston's suspicion vanished. "Of course, darling."

Chapter Fourteen:
Full of Surprises

After she managed to get rid of Winston, Julia hurried to us. At first she didn't believe our discovery. Then she was horrified. Then she was totally in. She grabbed her bike off the rack on her car.

"This is SO cool!" Julia exclaimed as we walked down the steps of the library toward our bicycles. "But I still can't believe Winston would just lie to me like that. It just doesn't seem right."

I could see the lighthouse easily from where I was, a constant reminder of my mission. "It's not right," I affirmed. "But he does not seem care about what's right. I think he was following us because I guess he thought we could help him...or maybe just because he was suspicious of us. Whatever he wanted, it looks like he found an easier route with you."

Julia sighed, appearing lost in thought. "I really thought things would work out...this time. But it looks like he's even worse than all the rest..." there was a catch in her voice. I glanced at her sympathetically and offered and kindly smile. She forced up a smile in return.

We reached the bicycle rack and started preparing our bikes to ride. Aunt Emma had dropped us and our bikes off at the pier with the assurance that, yes, we would meet her at the pier around five p.m. to go to dinner and then watch fireworks at dusk. I assured her we would be fine—we were both teenagers now, we were going to be together, and we both had our cell phones. However, it seemed time to make a subtle change of plans.

I whipped out my phone and dialed Aunt Emma. "Aunt Emma? Hi. Yes, we're done at the museum. Mmm-hmm. No, we were going to head over to the pier for a while. Is that okay? Oh…and we were going to go with someone we met. Well…what? Her name is Julia Anderson, and she works at the lighthouse. What?!?" Julia and Connor stared at me after this sudden exclamation, waiting for me to finish the conversation. "Well, isn't that something…okay. Thanks! Love you, too. Bye." I hung up the phone.

"What's up, Ethan?" Connor asked.

"Well, it seems that Aunt Emma knows Julia already," I replied.

Julia raised her eyebrows. "Wait…is this Mrs. Emma *Lewis*?" she asked. I nodded, and Julia continued. "We are both in a Saint Simons history and book club. I've known her for almost a year now. I think it's rather interesting that I have just run into her great-nephews!" Julia beamed, and I noted how quickly she seemed to have befriended us. She acted personable, pleasant…yet not overbearing. In less than half an hour, she had made us feel like old friends.

I grinned, mounting my bike. "And, of course, she gave us permission to go to the pier with you," I added. "So let's go!" I pedaled off, with Connor and Julia right behind me. This was shaping up to be a very interesting Fourth of July — a day full of surprises.

I was pedaling faster and faster, gliding across the sidewalk ahead of Connor and Julia. The breeze blew in my face and rustled the wispy, gray Spanish moss on the sidewalk ahead. The sun shone down upon the summer morning — warm, but not yet at its full heat. The massive trees diffused the light and cast curious, beautiful shadows all around. Suddenly, I felt a sense of unexplainable happiness. No matter what happened, I was happy.

Chapter Fifteen: Ludicrous

As we rounded the corner, we neared the building that contained the local library. Passing under a gnarled live oak, I slowed my pace and Julia pulled up beside me. She spoke precisely what I had been thinking.

"We can't do this on our own. It is simply ludicrous," Julia said forcefully.

"Thanks," I said, "Now I feel completely ludicrous."

Julia raised an eyebrow playfully. "You know what I mean! We can't just try to stop these thieves by ourselves."

"Is this foolish?" I asked thoughtfully.

She laughed. "I don't think so. But as Shakespeare put it, 'Better a witty fool than a foolish wit.' I think we ought to contact the police."

Connor, riding up behind us, butted in. "Great idea. Where's the police department?"

Julia shook her head slightly. "Frankly, I'm not sure. Probably in Brunswick. But navigating the roundabout is a pain, and there's really no need to go all the way there."

"Of course not...we could just call them," I agreed. I whipped out my phone. "Now we just need their number."

Julia had her phone already in hand. "A step ahead of you, Ethan."

Finding the number, she handed the phone to me. "This is your endeavor, anyway." Slowly I took the phone from her. I gulped as someone picked up the other line.

"Glynn County Police Department. How may we help you?"

"Umm...this is Ethan Lewis," I faltered, "I wanted to call and report a plot to vandalize the Saint Simons Lighthouse."

"Vandalism? What do you mean?"

"There are thieves who are planning to break into the lighthouse and steal some type of treasure that they believe is hidden there. From what I've gathered, they are going to do it tonight during the fireworks show."

"Hey, kid," the voice on the other end said reassuringly, "Don't worry about this kind of stuff. I can assure you that the lighthouse is perfectly safe."

"But wait! I know it's true...I have evidence! This is for real!" I protested.

"Oh...okay...well, we'll make sure to keep a lookout, " the man continued, "I'll make a note of this report, but we really don't have time for a wild goose chase. Thanks, and goodbye."

Dead silence.

I turned to Julia and Connor with a determined look, and they both read my face: we would do what was right, even if no one else would help...and even if it *was* ludicrous.

Still, one simple fact stood like a roadblock in our way. We needed more help. As I stood there silently brainstorming, a thought leapt into my head. I remembered my conversation with Cassidy, who had promised to help if she could. Perhaps she would be a valuable tool in dividing and conquering this mystery successfully.

So I made another phone call. Cassidy answered after it rang four times. "Hello, Ethan?"

"Hey, cousin," I greeted her. "What's up this fine Fourth of July morning?"

"Oh, nothing besides being my usual fantastic self! And what are you up to? Because I was thinking about that whole mystery you were talking about, and I *really* want to help. So…"

I cut her off. "Well, that's exactly why I called. We need backup. Things are getting tricky. We don't know exactly what to do, and we don't have much time, and—"

"All righty then! Can I meet ya'll somewhere? I'm in The Village right now, but my mom and her friend are taking foreeeevvver to shop—"

"Too long even for you?" I teased.

"—and…very funny, Ethan…and I can meet you if you're close."

"We're near the lighthouse, so we are pretty close to you. How about lunch?"

Cassidy agreed that lunch was a fantastic idea, so we set a place to meet her. She was certainly enthusiastic about the whole adventure—a little bit too enthusiastic perhaps—but she would still be incredibly helpful in our mission to save the lighthouse. I was sure of that.

Chapter Sixteen:
Third-Order Problem

When life hands you a lemon, you make lemonade. But what about when life hands you a green apple—something completely unexpected and unwanted? What do you do? Make sour apple juice?

I was in a difficult situation. The whole thing was growing beyond me. The various aspects of the plot—each a complicated enigma in itself—were tangled up in my mind. Even I was having doubts about my "foolproof" plan. Things needed to really start *happening*; for, if events did not swing quickly in our favor, all would be in vain.

I began to lay it all out: Winston, Ben, the Burnette Vanstory books, the haiku, the conversation on top of the lighthouse that fateful day which seemed so long ago...

Slurp! I was jolted from my glum reverie by Connor's loud drinking beside me. The three of us adventurers had stopped for lunch, and Aunt Emma would be joining us in a minute. Cassidy still hadn't arrived.

"Why can't you tell your aunt?" Julia asked, fingering her straw.

"I just...can't," I replied vaguely. "She might make us stop. She might tell us the same things that police officer told us. Then we'd be done for sure."

Julia shrugged, then her eyes flickered with amusement. "Whatever Winston is doing, he's up to no *gould*," she said, laughing at her own pun. I couldn't help but laugh as well, but Connor stared blankly at both of us with that flustered, trying-to-understand-the-inside-joke sort of look.

"What's so funny?" he asked.

"You know...James Gould built the first lighthouse...so, *good* and *gould*..." I explained. Connor nodded with a wry grin, then pointed out Aunt Emma walking toward us. She wore dangly red earrings that jingled when she walked.

"Hey there, Julia! Marvelous to see you!" she cried, sitting down beside me. "And boys, a very happy Independence Day to you!"

Hmm...Independence Day. One of the biggest days of the year on Saint Simons. One of the biggest days in the life of our country. Also, unbeknownst to the rest of the islanders, a big day in the history of the lighthouse—one that might affect its fate. I barely noticed when Aunt Emma gripped my hand and began to pray for our food.

"Dear God," she prayed, "Please bless this food, and those who made it, and please bless our time today. Thank you for our freedom and our history. In Christ's name I pray, Amen."

I wanted to tell her. I wanted her to pray for our situation. I wanted to scream, *The lighthouse is going to be vandalized, and we have to stop them, or it will be all my fault!* However, my lips seemed sealed shut.

My phone buzzed in my pocket. Pulling it out, I saw the text was from Julia: *The Fresnel lens in the lighthouse is a third-order lens. One of the bigger types of Fresnels.* I texted right back: *So?*

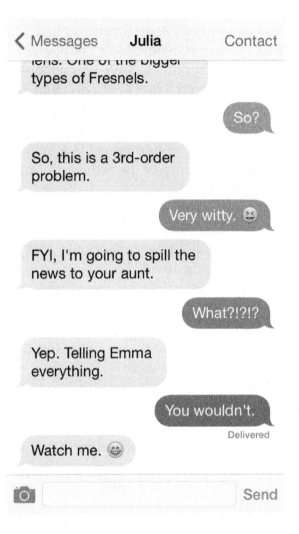

I glared hard at her across the table. Her only response was a prim, neat smile. Ignoring me, she turned to Aunt Emma.

"Emma," she began sweetly, tucking her hair behind her ear, "Have you noticed how lovely the lighthouse looks today?"

"I haven't been over there yet, but I'm sure it's

as beautiful as always!" Aunt Emma replied.

"But what if something happened to the lighthouse? Say — hypothetically, of course — someone vandalized it, defaced part of it, or stole something from it. How would you feel?"

Aunt Emma thought for a moment. "Well, I would be horrified. The lighthouse is a symbol of our beloved Island, and any of us would do anything to preserve its history."

Julia took a deep breath. "What if I told you that someone is planning to do all those things. Tonight."

Aunt Emma looked shocked and puzzled. "What are you talking about?"

I decided it was time for me to take over. "Two men are planning to break into the light and steal some type of treasure they believe is hidden there. We don't know exactly how or what they will do, but the three of us are determined to stop them."

"How do you know this?" she asked suspiciously.

"Because of this," I replied, handing her Winston's haiku, "and this", handing her the Burnette Vanstory clue.

"And this," Connor said, pulling up a few pictures of Winston and Ben at the various places we'd visited. They were incredibly blurry — but they got the point across to Aunt Emma. I looked at him in astonishment, because I hadn't known that he had been taking pictures all along. He grinned sheepishly.

"How?..." Aunt Emma's voice trailed off.

"They've been following us...because we know they are up to no good," put in Connor. "Ethan didn't want to tell you, but..." Aunt Emma narrowed her eyes at me.

"This is weird, but I suppose I have to believe you. First, let's call the police," she suggested.

"We already tried," Connor lamented. "No use. I don't think they really believed us."

"Well, here's one grown-up who will help you. Count me in!" Aunt Emma said.

"And me, too!" Cassidy announced, suddenly sitting down at the table. Then she paused, her blue eyes shining with curiosity. "What are we doing exactly?"

I grinned. This was — admittedly — the best thing that could happen. Aunt Emma and Cassidy would be much-needed support and backup.

Now it was time to put our plans into action.

"If Winston is looking for treasure in the lighthouse, what sort of treasure can it be?" Connor wondered aloud as we walked along the pier. It was a brilliant day, and the waves shimmered in the afternoon sun. I kicked at a clump of wet sand.

"I don't know," I replied. "He must be pretty sure it's in there, though, if he is trying to pull off this sort of stunt."

Julia looked thoughtful. "Well, what do you think is the most *valuable* thing about The Island?"

"Its history, perhaps," Cassidy suggested.

"Exactly what I was thinking!" said Julia. "I would wager that Winston is after some of the historic treasures in the lighthouse. It's simply full of them." She stopped walking and looked toward the lighthouse which now was behind us. "I think we can stop him. At least, we must try."

Julia was indubitably correct. Her idea was a logical one, and illuminated the whole situation a bit more clearly. However, the plan still seemed to stand rather precariously — go but a little awry, and all would fail.

The plan? I thought to myself suddenly. *What plan? Everything has changed. Things aren't shaping up how I thought.*

I knew we needed a plan — a new one, and one that would make use of all our newfound help. And who would have be the one to think up that new plan?

Yours truly, that's who.

Chapter Seventeen:
In Position

I walked in an aimless manner at the end of Mallery Street. With the pier behind me and the lighthouse in front, I was in perfect position to watch for Winston and Julia. My strategy was to be invisible by being in plain sight; after all, who would suspect an average teenager walking along the pier? Dozens of other people were picnicking on the lighthouse's lawn. Besides this, I had two things on my side: one, half The Island was gathered further down Mallery Street to watch the fireworks; and two, the sun was beginning to set, so it would be darker and easier to hide. No one would be focused on the lighthouse.

I turned down Beachview Drive, neared the lighthouse gift shop building, and went around the back side. I needed a place to hide, a place that would be in close proximity to the lighthouse and yet not close enough to be obvious. If I were conspicuous, then I might be found; if I were found, we would likely fail. For me, failing was not an option. My footsteps as I neared the far back edge of the building were soft and silent as feathers, yet also firmly determined. I crouched in the grass, in the same spot where Connor and I had been hiding only a few hours ago.

Sitting in the grass reminded me of my encounter with the sand flies in the marsh just two days earlier. I stood still, tapping my fingertips nervously, and looked toward the lighthouse. Our plan seemed foolproof, but now I was having doubts. What if someone forgot their job, or left their post?

Aunt Emma was not far from the lighthouse, seated among the crowd, prepared to watch the fireworks. What no one else knew was that she was watching for any sign of danger, ready to act at a moment's notice. Connor and Cassidy were stationed in between Aunt Emma and the lighthouse. My post was right near the lighthouse area, and Julia was waiting for Winston next to the light itself. We all had positions.

The positions made me think of playing the violin. Being a violinist myself, I knew how different hand positions worked: they were useful for getting notes in tune, but if you shifted slightly off, the note would sound terrible. Hopefully, our positions would work out fine.

Edging around the corner of the building, I observed that the coast was almost completely clear — much to my relief. I had seen police officers standing several blocks down as I walked to the light. For a brief moment, I felt bad about breaking rules, until I realized that these same police officers would be helping our cause within an hour.

It had taken some convincing to get Connor and Cassidy to be in their positions, as opposed to being with me by the lighthouse.

"It takes the adventure out of it!" Cassidy had protested. Connor, too, had been adamant about staying with me. But in the end they finally saw the sense of my plan and agreed to remain where I asked them to.

My phone buzzed in my pocket. I drew it out and read the text sent from Cassidy to Julia and me: *He's headed your way.* Sitting still as if I were frozen in time, I held my breath and waited. Although the distant crowd was noisy, all seemed — in an eerie way — quiet. My brain tuned out all other sounds as I focused in on that one noise I was waiting for.

Hearing footsteps, I listened carefully to a pretty voice on the other side of the brick edifice.

"Here we are," Julia said as she and Winston neared the light.

Little did anyone know that one of these persons was a thief, and the other was the only way to stop him. Julia and Winston went straight to the lighthouse. Julia had a key, and she unlocked the door quickly. Winston entered, and Julia paused, making sure to leave the door unlocked for me. She scanned the area briefly, her blue eyes darting to the place she knew I was hiding. With a subtle smile, she entered the keeper's dwelling which adjoined the lighthouse.

I crawled past the building's edge and hurried over to the light tower, hiding behind pillars and bushes along the way. No one noticed as I carefully slipped inside the keeper's dwelling, and the trickier part of our plan began.

Chapter Eighteen: Losing the Game

Winston was talking in a low voice, and I couldn't make out what he was saying. I moved down the dim hallway to where he and Julia stood, their backs to me.

"Good evening, my friends," I said. Even Julia started at my sudden statement. Winston jumped, a look of extreme surprise on his face. He settled down quickly and resumed his usual sneer. He took it all in stride, acting as if he was the utter master of the situation.

"Well, well, our little friend has come to join us, Julia!" he glared hard at me, still not realizing Julia's role in the situation.

Julia stepped away from Winston. "Of course—I invited him, you idiot."

Winston gasped sharply, now realizing that Julia had fooled him.

"How could you?" he demanded.

"How could *you*?" she retorted, her face twisted with angst. "Why? After all this time, coming back and lying to me and tricking me simply to find some treasure that may not even be there!"

Winston let loose a low, rumbling laugh like that of a rudely awakened giant. "Oh, it's there! And I plan to retrieve it without you!" He rushed at her and grabbed for the keys. Julia, thinking fast, ducked out of his way and tossed the keys to me. I snatched them out of midair and closed them between my palms. Winston rushed at me, enraged and certainly not amused at being turned into the monkey-in-the-middle. Barely having time to think, I dashed past him to the far end of the hallway. Winston approached me and held out his hand in a commanding manner.

"Hand over the keys, and this will be solved without any further difficulty," he ordered. I don't know what possessed me to do what I did next. I rushed at Winston and shoved him with all my might. Taken by surprise, he tripped and staggered backwards. I paused, not wanting to take things any further. Obviously Winston did not share my feelings. He sprang at me and shoved me firmly against a wall. I was surprised by his strength. I was pretty strong—I'd been weight training the whole school year before—but Winston's height and age gave him an advantage.

Thinking quickly, I kicked him in the shins and wrenched myself from his grip. He grunted and lunged for my left hand, which held the keys. They jingled as I pulled them out of his reach. His shirt slipped up, and I observed his belt and pockets—no gun. That, at least, abated some of my fears.

Julia had sneaked behind Winston unnoticed. So, as he hastily clawed at my hands, Julia swung at him with her purse, smacking him across the back of his head. Infuriated, he turned around and grabbed Julia's arm and twisted it.

"I've had quite enough of your antics," he growled, brutally gripping her arm.

That was the last straw. I formed a fist and punched him squarely in the jaw. Releasing Julia's arm, he reached for his face. His eyes narrowed. Then he delivered a punch that sent me reeling. In my haste to defend myself and fight back, I accidentally made a terrible mistake.

I dropped the keys.

They went sliding across the floor, and, before I could act, Winston grabbed them and ran madly toward the door which led to the tower. Julia and I could not stop him before he reached it.

"Don't you dare come another step closer!" he ordered.

"And enjoy your evening!" he called as he hastily ran up the stairs leading to the second floor of the keeper's dwelling. He locked the door solidly behind him.

Everything seemed to be collapsing. All we had worked for was for naught. Even if we did call the police, Winston might have already destroyed or defaced some part of the lighthouse. I shook my head.

Julia placed her hand on my shoulder. "Why so down? We've got a lighthouse to save!"

"But we can't now."

Julia smiled and produced something from her pocket. "Of course, I brought a spare set of keys. Come on—let's unlock the door."

She plunged the key into the lock, and it turned easily. The door opened, creaking, and we stared into the dim opening before us. It loomed like a great mouth that was waiting to swallow me up.

"Well," Julia looked at me. "This is where we split up."

I nodded. "Call the police. I think you have a pretty viable argument now...they have to believe you."

Julia readied her phone. "I'm calling them right now."

Then, hearing a voice behind us, we both whirled around to see a sight we neither expected nor wanted to see.

"Allow me," said Ben slyly, snapping a photo of the two of us. "The police ought to be aghast to find that you've been trespassing in the lighthouse."

"I work here," Julia glared at him, withdrawing the keys and stuffing them in her purse. "Nothing you can say will refute that."

"No," Ben shrugged. "But he doesn't work here, does he?" He pointed at me. "And the lighthouse is currently closed. Any normal person ought to be enjoying the fireworks, not secretly snooping around."

Ben pressed call and stepped just outside. Julia pursed her lips and narrowed her eyes. She said nothing, but I could see her lips mouthing *jerk*.

"Go," she whispered firmly. "Go stop Winston. I'll go after Ben."

"Are you kidding?" I asked. "I can't just leave you..."

"Go!" she demanded, then her tone softened. "Don't worry. I'll have plenty of help."

We turned and parted ways, both going toward equally desperate ventures.

With my phone's video camera on, I edged cautiously up the short flight of steps, not knowing when and where I would meet up with Winston. The sound of muffled footsteps came from behind one of many closed doors on the top landing. I edged over to the door, careful to make no loud sounds. It was then that I heard a strange whirring sound, accompanied by Winston talking in a low mutter to himself.

"There...that'll do," he mumbled almost silently,

and the whirring noise stopped. There was a crack and a click in the next room. Winston grunted, and the floorboards squeaked noisily beneath him — as if they were angry at him.

I started to push the key into the aged lock. A quick glance at my watch told me I would have very little time, and the fireworks show would be starting soon. The sky appeared a dim blue through the windows.

A scraping noise began in the adjoining room.

Then another noise: a jingling and clinking, almost like the links of a chain rattling together. Using the sound as a cover, I turned the key in the lock. It clicked. I took a deep breath and swung the door open. I took in everything quickly: the open backpack, the small electric saw, the removed floorboard.

"This is a public museum, you know. I don't think they'd appreciated you cutting through floorboards from the late 1800s," I said simply. Winston whirled to face me, a ghastly scowl on his face.

"How?" was all he said.

"I should ask you the same thing! How? How could you lie to Julia — your old friend? How could you do the thing you're doing right now? And why?"

He seemed more annoyed than terrified now. "Because, it involves money. People will do a lot for money, especially historic treasures."

"Even if you find what you're looking for, how will you get away? Any thoughts?" I stopped the video and quickly texted it to Cassidy.

"I have a lot of resources, kid. This is just a small project. Really — I have many routes, many plans, and many disguises. I can be out of here in a heartbeat."

I stood just outside the door. Winston glowered at me, holding his open backpack. Already he had something stuffed inside it—something that I could not get a adequate view of. I backed up a few steps, then surprised Winston by running back down the steps. I dashed down the hallway and stopped at the door. Hopefully I could alert the police...hopefully Julia and Connor would be back by now...

But Winston was not following me. I turned around and saw him fiddling with the door to the light tower. Finally opening it, he snatched up his backpack and began running to the lighthouse tower, beginning up the steps. I gasped and followed him as fast as I could on the winding stairwell.

The steps seemed to circle upwards forever. Dizzyingly they curved round and round as I charged up them.

Up, up, up.

129 movements of the feet.

I rushed out the door at the top, but didn't immediately see Winston. Blocking the door so he couldn't get out, I craned my neck to see which side of the upper platform he was on. However, the lens chamber obscured my eyes from seeing very far. I stiffened, holding my breath.

Nothing.

Quiet.

In the shadowy silence I heard no noise. For a long moment I stood still, my heart hammering in my chest, waiting for my adversary to show himself.

"Winston, this isn't funny!" I said. "Come out..or..."

"Looking for me?" he asked, stepping in from the shadows.

I was ready to end it all. My phone was out in a second. "I'm about to dial the police."

Winston pulled some papers and photos from his backpack. "If you do, I will burn these — the only proof that I'm the one responsible. It will be your word against mine." The papers included the itinerary I had made, which was Winston's clue for tracking us down.

"This is how we've been following you around, of course," he said. "We needed to explore this island and do a little research. Then you just had to show up and spoil our plans, didn't you?" He sneered. "I was suspicious of you, of course. But after that conversation you and your cousin had — I thought I had found my way into this lighthouse. Regrettably, I was wrong. You see, I really have nothing against you, and you should have nothing against me. We can pretend like this never happened." I tried to ignore him.

"What are you trying to do? What are you stealing?" I demanded.

"Would you like to know?" he demanded. "What do you think? What would I find hidden under the floorboards in a post-Civil War home? Use your brain, bookworm." I stood dumbfounded for a moment.

I had a few clues. A few sounds. All of them had come from behind that closed door.

The buzzing of the saw. The click as he pulled out the floorboard. And that peculiar jingle.

Winston spoke again, "You can't stop me, and you can't prove me wrong. So just quit it! Trust me, it won't be worth it for you." From his pocket he pulled out a handgun and gave me a good view of it, pointing it straight toward my widened eyes. I was shocked —

where had that come from? I braced myself.

"This lighthouse and its history—part of my home—not worth it? I don't think so," I said boldly. "The Island is worth the world to me." I tried to convince myself that the gun was simply a tool for threatening, and nothing more.

Winston sneered. "You are not going to win this!"

Suddenly, with a booming noise and burst of color, the first firework boomed off in the night sky. Cheering arose from the distant crowd. I tensed. When I turned to face Winston again, he held up the keys. They dangled from his pinching fingers.

"Here," he chuckled, "Catch!" He hurled the keys at me, and I grabbed for them, barely saving them from flying down to the ground below. I marveled at his carelessness with them, then realized what he was doing. He was stacking his evidence against me.

"The keys are all yours," he stated grimly. "You can keep them safe, or dispose of them. It's your choice...either way, the evidence is against you.

"Connor still has evidence. He has pictures," I retorted. "And I have this!" I pulled out the coded message. Winston was dumbfounded.

"How did you...?" he demanded.

"I have my ways," I said slyly. "Truly, I was given this message. It was dropped in my kayak just the other day."

Winston rolled his eyes. "Ben! That bumbling fool."

Winston shook his head in disgust. I commented slowly, "Maybe I will win this after all, eh?" Winston looked up and stared hard at me, not moving or making any motion. His eyes grabbed me with his disarming stare, and I stood, tense.

Then, with one swift motion, Winston threw

himself at me. He pinned my back against the iron railing and yanked the paper from my hand before I could stop him. I lunged and grabbed for it, but he shoved me backward, and I found myself leaning far over the railing. I tottered precariously.

The whole course of events seemed to be crashing down upon me. The wind whipped around my head. The dusky sky above was dim, as if it were a stage set for the colorful display that continued to explode in the distance. The breeze stung my eyes. I clenched my teeth. The wind stopped suddenly.

I gripped the iron rail until my knuckles were white as paper, and—with a shove—threw myself forward. I regained my footing and stood up.

Shaken by the incident, I glared at Winston, who now held the coded message—along with the other evidences he had threatened to burn. His eyes were already burning. They flickered in the evening lights.

Winston laughed in a way I hadn't heard him do before—it was the sort of laugh that says "I won."

"Oh, Ethan," he chortled, startling me by using my first name, "You don't even understand what's really going on." He pointed toward a police car that had pulled up down the street. Two figures were being led to the car. Although the light was dim, I instantly recognized them.

It was Connor and Julia.

Chapter Nineteen:
All the Cards Are Down

Winston was burning the final clues, but I barely noticed. Ben! It was now obvious that Ben had made sure Julia and Connor were found illegally trespassing. My eyes scanned the dim area near the sea. I saw no sign of Cassidy—could she have left her post? Why would she have? I knew the answer. She wanted the whole thing to be an adventure; she had said so multiple times. It seemed she had abandoned the plan.

And Aunt Emma? Nowhere in sight.

I was out of help, out of luck, and out of time.

Until now, I had been holding back. I had been restricting myself to the plan. However, the plan was failing fast, and something had to be done. I took in a deep breath and bolted through the open door and back down the stairs.

"Try to stop me!" I yelled behind me.

Winston followed in a flash. "There's nothing you can do now!"

"Maybe, and maybe not," I shouted.

"All you're doing is turning yourself in as a vandal," his voice sounded weird and echoing in the tower.

"So be it," I affirmed, stuffing the keys in my backpack as I reached the bottom of the stairs. There was no turning back now—all my cards were down, and I had no more choices. Still running, I pressed Aunt Emma's number in my contacts.

Buzzzzz.

I ran on.

Buzzzzz.

I ran, around the gift shop and onto the sidewalk.

Buzzzzz.

I ran, nearing the police car.

On the fourth ring, Aunt Emma picked up the phone. "Ethan?"

"Come to the lighthouse...now...hurry," I panted and hung up the phone.

Then, in my haste, I tripped and fell on the sidewalk. Time itself seemed to slow down as I fumbled and grabbed wildly, but to no avail. My phone fell and crashed into the pavement, and I heard the sound of glass shattering.

I picked the phone up quickly, glancing over my shoulder to see Winston just looking out of the lighthouse door. My phone's glass screen was cracked terribly, and it had flickered out to a blank nothingness. Why, oh why, had I taken off the case?

This adventure was getting pretty bleak. It wasn't half the exciting escapade I had imagined. Instead, it seemed that all the odds were turning against me.

Aghast, I hurried on toward the police car with Winston closing in behind.

The police didn't really believe my story, especially since Winston arrived but a minute after I did — and since Ben was already there. From Winston's tale, I was simply a young vandal messing around with the lighthouse. Winston had been "chasing me out of the restricted property." The policemen searched my backpack and found the telltale evidence — the keys — just as Winston had hoped.

"It's not true," I protested.

"But you are working with these two" — here the officer motioned to the car containing Julia and Connor — "and they were sneaking around, too. And the fact that there were keys in *your* backpack and *her* purse...I'm afraid you have no excuse."

"They were trying to stop them!" I said, pointing to Winston and Ben.

"Can you prove it?" the officer stated simply.

I hung my head. "Five minutes ago I could have. But he burned the clues and stole the rest."

Winston shrugged.

"If you have no proof, I can't really take a teenager's word over an adult's. We'll have to do some further investigation." the officer obviously wasn't convinced by my explanation.

"Wait...Connor has pictures," I put in hastily.

"He already showed those pictures to us," the officer said exasperatedly. "They're so blurry it's impossible to identify anyone. I can't take such inconclusive evidence."

Connor was banging on the car window — quite vehemently. He was pressing against the window a tiny fragment of paper that I didn't recognize at first. Then, with a shock of joy, I realized what it was. It was the haiku note.

Chapter Twenty:
Proof

"They're making this up! He probably wrote this just now." Winston protested a second time. "That doesn't even look like my handwriting!"

I figured I had won. But the officer simply looked at me and said, "This isn't enough. I need real proof. Plus, your friend did have a pen in his pocket, so the evidence is still against you." I shook my head in despair and disgust at Winston, the police, and the whole situation. *Where is Aunt Emma?* I thought. I knew even my carefully kept notebook would be of no use.

Julia's eyes met mine and I saw a reflection of what I felt.

"I know what he's stealing!" I announced. "Money! He's stealing money."

One of the policemen rolled his eyes. The officer who appeared to be in charge sighed firmly. "Look, man, this guy isn't stealing anything. I think that's pretty clear."

Winston edged out of the center of the group. "If you'll excuse me, I'd like to go enjoy the...fireworks," he said.

"All right, sir," the policeman said, "but I need your name and phone number, and I need to see your driver's license."

Winston spouted out a number, then said, "My name is James Wyly. W-y-l-y." I was truly angry now. Winston had stalked us, lied to Julia, damaged a historical monument, and fibbed to a police officer. My face burned with fury; my teeth gritted together. A red burst of light boomed in the distance. Winston, slipping a license (presumably fake) back into his wallet, turned to leave.

"He has a gun," I offered, grasping for some final evidence. Winston's eyes widened. Ben visibly tensed, and their eyes met in a moment of uncanny understanding.

The officer's hand went to his own weapon. "Is this true?" he calmly questioned Winston.

"Nope," Winston said, pulling up the edge of his shirt. His belt held no gun. I gasped, and looked from Winston to the policeman. *How?* I thought.

Winston smirked at me, then shrugged his shoulders. "Kid, stop trying to get yourself out of this. The proof is against you."

"Wait!" Cassidy shouted testily, running up behind us. "I have the proof you need!" Surprised, I smiled at her, realizing she hadn't really deserted the plan.

Ben looked around at the unfolding scene about him, his eyes bulging. Winston looked like he was going to run for it. A swift police officer stepped in his way and nodded at me and Cassidy, waiting. Cassidy pulled out her phone, turned it on, and pressed play on the most recent video. It was the video of Winston in the lighthouse. The video of him sawing at the floorboards in the keeper's dwelling. It was the solution.

It was proof.

If the video didn't convince the policeman, they certainly were convinced when they saw for themselves the damaged floorboard. Winston was given Connor and Julia's former seat in the police car, and that was the last I saw of him and Ben. Inside that black Honda that had followed us around like an ominous shadow, the police found Winston's backpack. Inside it was his gun—and the stolen objects. They clinked. They jingled.

Coins. Dozens of them sloshed around in that aged leather pouch. Some were simply old pennies, quarters, and nickels. However, most were genuine Confederate coins, still practically in mint condition. Those were valuable relics indeed.

Despite what it had seemed at first, Cassidy had not abandoned the plan on purpose. She had been forced to.

She and Connor had watched and waited. However, around the time Ben was sneaking up on me and Julia, Cassidy had been spotted by several of her friends from dance camp. Not wanting to make Connor's hiding spot known, she had gone over to her friends and chatted with them to keep them occupied— and to keep all attention away from the lighthouse. Thus, when Connor had seen Ben assaulting Julia and dashed to her aid, Cassidy had not followed him. She decided her role was to keep our endeavors a secret. Yet when she received my video, she knew she had to act. Getting rid of her friends with a hastily contrived excuse, she had acted as if she were heading for the restrooms near the lighthouse. In truth, she was coming to our rescue. She had arrived just barely in time.

Long afterwards, the detectives were able to uncover some of what Winston had been doing. Before long I knew a couple of things: he was some sort of treasure hunter, and he had been using a lot of false information—much as I had suspected. Winston, as I knew him, was not actually named Winston. His real name has remained a mystery to us all. This incident was not the first in his track record, it seemed. He was a thief, a thief who would have tried to steal a little bit of the lighthouse. I suppose he hadn't bargained that someone would stop him. Yet Connor and I had—and Julia and Cassidy, too. We had stopped the lighthouse thief.

Aunt Emma arrived on the scene just in time to congratulate me, and a police officer was with her. She had spotted him standing several yards away from her, and, after a lengthy explanation, had convinced him to come to the lighthouse. While the police finished investigating the light, we were all allowed to climb to the top. It was the third time that week I had done so, but this time was different.

Connor stood beside me. Neither of us spoke a word. We didn't have to.

In the distance, I saw the final fireworks exploding like colorful cannons. I couldn't help but feel they were shot just for me.

Chapter Twenty-one:
Home

The next two days were spent in blissful holiday. An article in the newspaper—granted, a very small article—had been written about our doings to save the lighthouse. It was a short blurb, but it was there nonetheless. The police were, of course, beginning to look into Winston's case. I was content, knowing the lighthouse was now safe.

Amidst all the celebration, I sat down to read a book. It was only thirty-one pages long, but it was one of the best books I have ever read. *Saint Simons Island* by Burnette Lightle Vanstory expressed in so many ways how I feel about Saint Simons Island. If I could have met Mrs. Vanstory, I think we would have been the best of friends. She understood The Island; she understood the "treasure that rust does not corrupt nor thieves break in and steal;" she understood that "ours is a goodly heritage."

One passage in particular summed up my feelings:

> To those of us who love St. Simons, there is an indefinable charm about it that simply can't be put into words. There is no doubt in our minds that The Island is our Very Most Favorite Place, but when pressed for a reason, we are at a loss for an answer. Pondering awhile, we decide, "There's just something about it." Our questioners say, helpfully, "I suppose the bathing beach is wonderful." We hasten to

assure them that the beach is not considered as good as many others. "Good surf?" We admit that we have seen better. "Is the water that heavenly blue you see in Florida?" We explain that it is often quite brownish—so many rivers flow into the ocean there, you know. "Good fishing?" Best there is if you hit it right and know where to fish—not much deep-sea fishing, though. "Cool in summer, I'll bet!" We confess that it can get the hottest of any place we ever saw when the breeze dies down. At this point, our questioner usually gets rather a baffled look, and we grin and say, "There's just something about it."

Even I couldn't put my finger on what that "something" was. Perhaps it was the places. Perhaps it was the people. Perhaps it was the history. Whatever it was, it summed up those four reasons why I loved Saint Simons.

My parents arrived on Thursday, and Connor was going back to Chicago the same day. Julia, Cassidy, and Aunt Emma all came to the airport to say goodbye to Connor and greet my parents. From my parents' faces, I knew they had a lot of exciting things to tell about their trip. I had more to tell, though.

"Ethan!" my mom said with a smile the moment they arrived in the terminal. "We missed you! Did you miss us, though, is the question?" she laughed.

"Well...I did miss you, but I was a bit busy to think about it," I admitted.

"What were you busy with?" she asked curiously.

Aunt Emma came up to us. "Read for yourself!"

Glancing over the newspaper, Mom's eyes widened. She read and reread sentences. When she finished, then stared at Aunt Emma and I with an astonished look. "So this is what you all do when I leave?" she teased.

"What's up?" Dad asked, walking over to the group and pulling their luggage behind.

"It's a long story," I grinned. Connor tapped my shoulder.

"Ethan, I have to leave now," he said quietly. I sighed. Connor had transformed from bother to cousin to friend to brother, all in one week. It was difficult to let him go, now that I had seen what having a brother was really like. I put out my hand to shake his, but instead he pulled me in for a hug.

I was surprised. Connor didn't seem to be the hugging type.

I pulled something from my backpack and handed it to Connor. "A bottle of Coke — for while you wait on your flight. Don't drink too many, pig." Connor grinned broadly. "Oh...here," I said, pulling out the lighthouse keychain my mom gave me, "I want you to have this." He accepted the gift and transferred it to his own pocket.

"Thanks, Ethan," he said genuinely, "Thanks for everything. This has been so much fun." He smiled. "I think I understand the fourth reason why you love Saint Simons now. I just wish I could stay here longer."

I shook my head and smiled. "There's an old saying that if you get Saint Simons sand in your shoes, you will be itching to come back. I'm sure you will be back here." I paused. "And of course, we'll keep in touch." I tapped my phone in my pocket.

"Goodbye, Ethan," he said, and turned to head toward the loading station. I felt a catch in my throat as I watched him leave.

I told Mom and Dad the whole story, and they decided the occasion deserved a trip to CJ's Pizza. I wholeheartedly agreed. Riding in Julia's car on the way there, I looked out the window. We were just passing over the bridge that connected the mainland to The Island. I could see the marshlands stretching out on either side, with live oaks lining the roads.

I was home.

Author's Notes

Ever since I was born, I've spent Fourth of July week at my grandparents' house on Saint Simons Island, Georgia. Those weeks of fun and wonder left me with a deep collection of memories of the beauty and grandeur of The Island.

Thus, this is a book not only steeped in The Island's rich history, but in my own experiences. Many things Ethan and Connor encounter—the sand flies in the marsh, horrific heat at Fort Frederica—are almost autobiographical for me.

Obviously, I'm incredibly thankful to my amazing grandparents Jim and Alva Youngner for having my family and my cousins' family down at their house every Fourth of July. Each visit to Saint Simons is amazing, and they make it even more extraordinary.

To my mom and my sisters Kendall and Courtney who read and reread (and reread) the book as it progressed through various stages of editorial development, thank you. I certainly could not have finished this on my own.

To Josiah Dooley, my amazingly talented illustrator: I simply can't express how grateful I am for your help. God has gifted you in fantastic ways. Thanks for always putting up with each and every one of my nitpicky suggestions!

To the others who read the book as a second pair of eyes—my "guinea pig" test audience: thanks to my sister Kelley, cousin Isabella, and friend Kit. You are priceless.

Above all, thanks to God, who provided each and every person, idea, book, material, and circumstance that produced this book.

CPSIA information can be obtained at www.ICGtesting.com
Printed in the USA
BVOW06s1438051015

421030BV00022B/92/P